The Boyhood of Cain

The
Boyhood
of Cain

MICHAEL AMHERST

RIVERHEAD BOOKS

NEW YORK

2025

RIVERHEAD BOOKS
An imprint of Penguin Random House LLC
1745 Broadway, New York, NY 10019
penguinrandomhouse.com

First published in hardcover in Great Britain by
Faber & Faber Ltd., in London, in 2025
First United States edition published by Riverhead, 2025

Book design by Amanda Dewey

Library of Congress Cataloging-in-Publication Data

Names: Amherst, Michael, author.
Title: The boyhood of Cain / Michael Amherst.
Description: New York : Riverhead Books, 2025.
Identifiers: LCCN 2024042588 (print) | LCCN 2024042589 (ebook) |
ISBN 9780593718520 (hardcover) | ISBN 9780593718544 (ebook)
Subjects: LCGFT: Bildungsromans. | Novels.
Classification: LCC PR6101.M44 B69 2025 (print) |
LCC PR6101.M44 (ebook) | DDC 823/.92—dc23/eng/20240920
LC record available at https://lccn.loc.gov/2024042588
LC ebook record available at https://lccn.loc.gov/2024042589

Printed in the United States of America
1st Printing

The authorized representative in the EU for product safety and compliance is
Penguin Random House Ireland, Morrison Chambers, 32 Nassau Street,
Dublin D02 YH68, Ireland, https://eu-contact.penguin.ie.

For my parents: Miles and Jane,
and also Diana

In the religion of the once-born the world is a sort of rectilinear or one-storied affair, whose accounts are kept in one denomination, whose parts have just the values which naturally they appear to have, and of which a simple algebraic sum of pluses and minuses will give the total worth. Happiness and religious peace consist in living on the plus side of the account. In the religion of the twice-born, on the other hand, the world is a double-storied mystery. Peace cannot be reached by the simple addition of pluses and elimination of minuses from life. Natural good is not simply insufficient in amount and transient, there lurks a falsity in its very being.

WILLIAM JAMES,
The Varieties of Religious Experience

The Boyhood of Cain

.

Chapter 1

They live in a large house near the grounds of the choir school, where his father is headmaster. The school, a preparatory school, is situated in the center of town. The main building is big, red brick like a doll's house, shadowed by the Norman tower of the town's abbey. The rest of the school is made up of former houses that line one of the town's three main streets. These streets meet at a stone cross in the town's center, erected in memory of the townspeople who died in the wars.

Neither of his grandfathers fought, on account of their poor eyesight, and the fact his family did not do their bit brings him shame. When the other boys in his year boast of their grandfathers' heroics in the army, navy or air force, he must keep quiet. His father did national service, but rather than killing Germans he played in a brass band and catered in the officers' mess. Perhaps his family are cowards.

As well as three roads, the town also has three rivers. Every winter these rivers break their banks and flood the surrounding fields. In summer, the flood-plain grows thick with lush green grass. In this way, the town is open and expansive in summer, while becoming hemmed in and dark with the water surrounding it from all sides in winter.

Every morning, unless his father has choir practice, he and his sister make the short walk with him from their front door, along Church Street and into the school. Later, when he remembers this, he has an image of them walking together, his own hand small and warm in his father's fist, his father carrying an umbrella and swinging it like the gentlemen in films. But this is a false image, or false memory, because his father is too forgetful to ever keep an umbrella for more than twenty-four hours.

Similarly, he imagines his father in a suit and people touching their foreheads in a little bow as they go by. But this is also false. His father always wears thick, plaid shirts, with one button unwinding on its thread. The only thing that is true is his own pride at the warmth and greetings that fall on his father, and by extension himself, when they're in town. This makes them a pre-eminent family—the first family. But then maybe that is every family's sense of itself.

Will the school also form part of his inheritance, one day? he wonders. His father is reticent about this, but surely if the school is his father's, then, like everything else—like the clock his father says has been in the family for generations and one day will be his—the school will also become his own.

As the headmaster's son he is in a unique position. Unlike his sister, who is embarrassed by her special status, he raises it with classmates often. Yet, the more he mentions it, the less they seem to like him. When the other children, particularly the boys, boast and square up to each other over their fathers' jobs, he does not see why his own father's should be a source of suspicion rather than pride.

His father does not teach him, he only teaches the top two forms. However, sometimes he will see his father around school. When he does, he waits for a sign, an acknowledgment that he is his son, a sign that he is special.

But his father does not acknowledge him in this way, no sign is forthcoming. He wants his father to lay claim to him. But he will not. His mother, on the other hand, is always happy to claim him as her own. She will call to him, wave to him at the school gates. She will lie to get him out of school or off games. His mother claims him to a degree that is humiliating.

The only time he is his father's son is when his mother cannot collect him from school. On these days, he is permitted to go through the red double doors of the main school building, the doors only to be used by teachers, and to wait on the long settle in the hall for his father to finish teaching. He is unique among the children in being able to use these doors, in being able to access the school at weekends, and in being able to walk up the staff staircase, which is made of marble and sweeps in a curve up to the landing.

It only occurs to him how arbitrary it is to forbid the use of a set of doors one Monday morning, when he is running an errand during class and is caught going through them by the games master. He does not see why he should be able to use the doors at weekends with his father but not during the week. He can use these doors, the staff staircase, because he is his father's son. To deny him is in some way to deny his father. And yet, after the games master tells him that it is not the weekend, so he cannot go that way, he accepts: his fear of being bad is greater even than his sense of his own importance.

He dare not say that this is a stupid rule. He is yet to see any sign that the teachers possess some quality in relation to doors that he does not. All he feels is how much he wishes he were with his father all the time. With his father he can go anywhere.

One day, while waiting for his father to finish the last lesson of the afternoon, he's taken to the top of the school, where his father teaches maths. The ceilings on the upper floor are lower and each of the rooms is lit by long strip lighting that emits a low-level buzz. His father's classroom is dim and airless. The boy stands next to him at the front, while his father draws in chalk on the blackboard. The floor is covered with a dark brown vinyl that is breaking up in places to reveal the boards beneath. The boys are lined up behind desks. But these are not boys, they are all thirteen, or nearly thirteen, and they have the long limbs of men. Some even have men's voices. He cannot imagine ever being as old as they are.

When the bell goes, he and his father are left alone. With the school quiet and empty, he feels the place belongs to his father and, as a result, it must belong to him also. They walk down to his father's study, past wall displays in French and drawings of trees. He knows the words are French, although he has not yet learned what they mean; he can make his own drawings of trees but has not yet learned how to reproduce them so beautifully.

Next to the study door, there is a large wooden cupboard, which his father opens with a small key. Inside are packs and packs of shrink-wrapped exercise books. These are the books they use in class, each covered with pastel shades of sugar paper. Dark teal green with squares for maths, yellow with wide-ruled lines for his year group, pink-orange with narrower lines for use by the older children. His father takes one and then asks if he'd like some too.

Receiving a new exercise book is one of his chief joys. Whenever one of his classmates finishes their book and puts a hand up to say they need a new one, a hush covers the room. If he had bigger, messier handwriting he would get a new book more often. He feels it an injustice that he should be punished for having a better, tidier script.

The new books are stiffly bound, with shiny covers. Over time, their binding grows weaker, the pages dirty, and the sheen disappears. In the first lessons after receiving a new book, he will write smaller, more neatly, ensuring that every letter sticks to the line. Every time he harbors some hope that this time will be different: *this* time he will reach the end with no errors at all.

However, he knows that no matter how careful, no matter how well-meaning he is, he will make crossings out. When he misspells a word, he is torn between two equally bad choices: to cross it out and correct it, leaving messy evidence of his mistake, or carrying on regardless, but with the mistake there for all to find.

To make an error on the clean, white pages of a new exercise book feels, to him, a terrible sin. He wants to leave no trace or, at least, no trace of his own fault. It would be better to have written nothing than to leave signs of error.

When his father opens the cupboard to reveal a wall of such books, he cannot believe it. And when he casually grabs a couple of each of the exercise books and hands them to him, he is dumbfounded. He opens one and then another, smells the sickly release of glue and fresh paper.

His father asks what he will use them for, to which he replies, "Stories." He does not have any stories to tell, he cannot think of any, but he likes the idea of filling the pages, writing a book of his own, like the ones he reads in the evenings at home. He would like to write a story that carries all the way to the end.

He tries to prolong their stay here because this is the happiest he can ever remember being. Here he has access to all he could want. When they finally descend the stairs to the staff car park it is with the knowledge that he is his father's son.

Chapter 2

In class, the teacher, Mrs. Walters, tells them animals can see only in black and white.

"What about my cat?" he asks.

"All cats," she tells them.

"So what about my uniform? Can they—"

"It would all be black and white," she says. "Black, white and gray."

Throughout the rest of the lesson, they are given three photographs, which they must copy onto pieces of paper. He has a picture of a family, one of a cat and dog, and finally an owl in a tree. They are told they must draw each of these out twice, and color them in—once as they see it, and once as animals see it. The teacher shows them how deep reds and blues will become almost black, while the light tones of skin, pale pinks and yellows will appear gray or almost white.

Midway through he puts his hand up to ask a question.

"Also, some people are color-blind," he says.

"Yes," responds the teacher.

"And animals only see black and white."

"Yes."

"So how do we know what the real color is?"

The teacher doesn't understand the question.

"Well, we might see the sky as blue and a cat might see it as gray, but really it might be green," he says.

"I don't think so," she responds, and she makes her way down the aisle of desks.

He puts his hand up again. But the teacher does not respond or pretends not to see. Eventually, desperate, he calls out: "But we don't know. What if the animals are right? What if everything is only gray?"

The girl sat in front of him tells him to shut up, before covering her work with a hand. Maybe she thinks he is showing off.

"I don't believe, if everything were only gray, we would be able to see all the other colors," the teacher tells him, crossing her arms across her breast. "If we can see all the colors—all the extra colors—then they must be there. While the animals can only see two colors—black and white, and the two mixed together as shades of gray."

The boy thinks again.

"Maybe there are lots of other colors," he begins. "Other colors we can't see. Maybe the grass is blue and the sky is green. What if—"

"Look," the teacher finally says. "I don't think any of this is very helpful. You've been given the exercise and you are to get on with it. Everyone else is getting on with it, why can't you?"

"But what if—"

"I've told you what the colors are," she snaps. "You know what the task is. Everyone else is getting on quietly. Now I advise you to do the same."

He becomes quiet. One boy turns and glowers at him. But he worries about his cat. He would like his cat to see in color. He feels sorry for his cat if she cannot. At home, he lies on his front, across the carpet, and stares into her yellow eyes, hoping she might reveal the truth.

He hopes Mrs. Walters is wrong. He hopes only some animals cannot see colors. But above all he wants to know what color things *truly* are. He worries. He does not know what the teacher means by green; it may mean something different when he sees it to when his mother sees it. What if green for him is blue for his mother? What if no one sees the same thing? What then? And why does no one care?

❧

He has had discussions like this with his mother. He will demand answers from her that she either does not know or refuses to give. Chief among them is the question of why he must go to school. He has never wanted to go to school. He knows that everyone must go, but this does not seem a sufficient reason. He does not know why he can't do what he likes. There was a time when he stayed at home all day with his mother. He cannot see why this should have changed. He can't understand what would force a child to leave his parents and their home. He recognizes school as a first step, the first in a series of moves he does not wish to make.

His mother reprimands him, "Soon, Daniel, you will realize there are things you simply have to accept. You cannot just will things different because you don't like them as they are. Some things you just have to get on with."

If he were Jesus then he would never have to go to school. The subject of his being Jesus has come up before. When he was younger his mother would come and sit on the end of his bed and talk or sing to him while stroking the hair from his forehead. She would run a finger around his palm, before trailing it up to the crook of his elbow, and then back down again. She would wait until he fell asleep and then he would wake to find her gone, his arm cold above the duvet.

On one of these nights, as his mother sits and tries to brush the frown from his brow, he challenges her, "Why do I have to go to school?"

"Because everyone goes to school," she replies.

"But I don't have to."

"Yes, you do, everyone has to."

"Why?"

"Because that's the way it is."

This does not satisfy him as an answer.

"But why?"

"Well, you need to go to school so you can learn things and get a job."

"But I don't want a job."

She laughs.

"Most people don't want a job," she tells him.

He finds this answer silly. If no one wants a job, then surely no one should have one. As far as he can see, the point of being an adult is that you no longer have to do things you don't want to do. That is the only good thing about it.

Being grown up means an end to play and he wants to keep playing. Why do you have to become anything, instead of just playing at it? One day he'd like to be a teacher and the next day a train driver. As an adult this should be possible, but it would seem it is not.

"Why do I have to have one? Why does anyone have one, if no one wants one?"

"So you can earn money to buy food and to be able to look after yourself. And your family," she adds. She takes her hand away from his forehead and holds it in her lap.

"But I don't have a family."

"But you will one day."

"Why can't I just stay here? Why can't I just stay here with you? You can look after me. Then I won't need a job."

"But we won't be around forever."

His mother has taken to saying this, it seems, whenever she does not know the answer to one of his questions. She summons up a time when he will be on his
own. This upsets him, this far-off place that will take
away his parents. But in that moment, he does not want
to get distracted from the task in hand. He is ready to
compromise.

"Well, until then."

"Until then what?"

"Until then I can stay with you and Daddy. Here. So I
won't need a job and I won't need to go to school."

She sighs.

"You still need to go to school," she begins again.

"But why?"

"So you can meet people and have friends."

"But I don't want friends."

"So you can meet someone and get married and have
a family of your own."

He looks at her. None of this seems very likely. Is that
all that is to happen? Are people born, have jobs, have a
family, then die? Is this it? He feels she must be holding
something back.

"If I were Jesus," he says, "I could make it so I didn't
have to go to school."

"If you were Jesus," his mother tells him, "you would
know."

"Maybe I do know," he says cryptically. He knows
enough to have asked, he reckons, to have had the

thought. Jesus cannot have known he was the Son of God. If he did, he would have been an insufferable child, a difficult adolescent. To have told the other children you were the Son of God would demand a certain amount of bullying. He has learned from school that boasting of his father's status does not endear him to the other children. How much worse would it have been for the carpenter's son. Jesus cannot have been told, his parents would have been too wise for that.

Jesus must have found the realization of his special nature growing within him. Neither does he believe Mary would have randomly told him one day—how then would Jesus have believed it? What would have happened to his relationship with Joseph? So no, he reckons that, like himself, Jesus must have started simply by asking the question: am I the Son of God? And that, like him, his mother would have told him to stop being so silly, until eventually the inevitable overcame them both.

Maybe, he reasons, his mother, like Mary, has been dreading this day and has had her lies prepared. Or maybe his mother genuinely doesn't know. Maybe his question has caught her by surprise? Either way, he would like her to have been better pleased.

Chapter 3

His father is sick. His left leg has swollen to twice the size of the right. He can't walk, he can't go into school, he can't even climb the stairs of their house. Instead, he must lie on the sofa in the living room, which it turns out can be pulled out into a makeshift bed. The cat hides under its larger frame and their father curses whenever it jumps on him. This way his father now occupies the living room, depriving him and his sister of access to the television set.

Each morning they will sit on the edge of their father's downstairs-bed and talk with him, while the television is shut away. They pretend that this is fine but secretly they resent that their father has taken over the house.

As he is unable to work, he is now here at all times as well. The children are confined to their bedrooms. The boy does not know how their father has engineered this:

in one swift movement he has gone from being absent to a constant presence, from subsidiary to their mother to ordering her about and asking for her help. She now has less time for him and his sister. Even when she takes them to school it is in a hurry before returning home for the doctor.

At the back of his mind, he wonders if his father will die. His father is older than those of other boys. He is twenty years older than their mother. His mother has always told both him and his sister that they should be prepared for their father dying.

"He will die," she says, "before your friends' fathers. He will die when their grandparents die. You should be prepared for this."

A boy in his year, Yanis, has lost his father. Everyone knows this but there is a silent agreement that no one should ever speak of it. Shortly after Yanis was born his father's boat was discovered overturned but a body was never found. He wonders whether Yanis has made the story up.

However, when he goes to Yanis's house, on a day his own mother cannot collect him from school, he can find no sign of a father—there are not even any photos of him. He has a sense of something missing, a house only half-full. Yet, at the same time, he feels Yanis's father everywhere—always at one remove, always hiding in the next room.

Perhaps Yanis's father has run away and is leading a new life somewhere else? He half expects to see him standing in the doorway and Yanis's deception revealed. Either way, it seems there is little to be gained by losing your father. If it does confer a special status on Yanis, then it is not one he can make use of.

He understands that his father's illness is the least of their problems. This is what his mother says, tired and strained one evening, running the iron over clothes with the same swift motion his teacher uses to guillotine worksheets. The school has built a new sports hall, but it has overshot the budget, she explains. They will have to move; they will have to sell their home.

Will his father go to prison, the boy asks. She assures him he will not. But he is not so sure. He has seen films, read in books, that fathers who get into trouble with money are sent to prison. He knows the story of *The Railway Children* inside out. He does not understand how his father—the big man about town—can be short of money.

It seems the problem is made worse by his father also letting parents off paying their fees. He is owed money but does not wish to call in the debt. If this carries on, the school will close. He asks why these people cannot pay their fees and his mother tells him it is because they are poor. Or rather, they *claim* to be poor.

She tells him about one parent, Mrs. Fletcher, who had seen his father a few weeks ago to tell him that she would be forced to withdraw her two children from the school. His father felt sorry for her and told her not to worry—she could begin to pay the fees again when she felt able. However, the school secretary saw Mrs. Fletcher in Cheltenham, two weeks later, buying clothes from a boutique in Montpellier. Unable to decide between two dresses, the secretary overheard Mrs. Fletcher resolve to have them both. The vigor of his mother's ironing increases as she tells this, against the chatter of the radio on the window ledge.

His father is annoyed at this deception but will not say anything. The boy feels his parents are being unfair. Maybe Mrs. Fletcher really is very poor but is only buying the dresses to cheer herself up? Why are his parents so suspicious and uncharitable?

Besides, if anyone is to blame for the situation with Mrs. Fletcher it is his father. It is his father who agreed to let her off the fees, his father who will not say anything now, and his father who waives his right to money without considering the impact on the school or his own family. If Mrs. Fletcher, and others, have found his father a soft touch it only exposes his father's lack of judgment.

His father makes a habit of giving money away. Indeed, if his father has any job, it seems to consist of giving away as much of his money as he can, as quickly as he can. Whenever he has made someone a gift of money, he will always confide it to the family afterward.

"My father, your grandfather," he explains, "always said, 'Never lend anything you cannot afford to give.' He gave lots of people money, yet he made a point of never telling anyone. No one ever knew."

The boy points out that his father is not following his own father's example. Unlike his grandfather, his father always tells them afterward; he is incapable of keeping a confidence. Worse still, he is only doing it to swell his own pride.

It frustrates the boy that his father does not care about the right things. He could be a great man, yet he refuses to take up his rightful place. He behaves in ways that do not accord with his status. When strangers greet them in the street, the boy is embarrassed as his father exclaims loudly, "I have no idea who that is!"

"But, Daddy, they can hear you," he will say.

He does not want them to hear, for he doesn't want them to think ill of his father. He likes that people want to be known to them and he feels this to be an advantage that should not be given away. Only his father doesn't seem to care.

What he would like is for these people to look up to his father all the time. Yet being known around town is a double-edged sword. Behind their affection the boy suspects there lurks something else—that they laugh behind his father's back: not only do strangers smile and nod in their direction as they walk down the high street, but he has seen the looks they give when his father necks his third pint in the pub before lunch. In this way, at least, they look down on him. The boy hates them for this. Nearly as much as he hates his father, for giving so much away.

His father rarely spends money on the family and almost never on anything new, unlike some of the children at school, whose parents spoil them with computer games and trips abroad to Disney World. Any money his father has seems to be tied up in the school. He would rather this were not the case. If his father is a rich man, then he should behave like one—family holidays, a new car—rather than making do with cast-offs and deals he does down the pub.

It is almost as if his father is ashamed of having money, which is perhaps why he's in such a hurry to give it away. He blames this on the fact that his father only wants people to like him. He does not care for the good opinion of his family, the only people that matter, but for the approval of other men—the surly, quiet men in the pub, whose approval he buys with loans and drinks. As far as the boy is concerned, this makes him a poor example of a man. He knows from myths and legends that a man should earn his reputation through his deeds. He should be indifferent as to whether this will gain him anything in the minds of others. A poor man is one solely concerned with currying favor.

✺

Owing to his illness, it is agreed his father will take early retirement. He will cease to be headmaster and they must sell the large house and move out of the town. The loss of their home is like a death. Yet his parents claim their move is not merely for financial reasons. They plan to move to the countryside and keep animals—it is to be an entirely new way of life. Their model is a sitcom with Richard Briers and Felicity Kendal, although he disapproves of his parents making decisions based on aping characters off the telly.

What this means is that he will cease to be the headmaster's son. He will no longer get to walk with his father through town, his cheek rubbing against the tweed of his father's sleeve. He fears people will no longer know who his father is. To him, their reduced status is a form of disgrace.

His mother does all the packing, which she does without complaint. For this the boy is grateful, while counting it against his father. While she hurries inside and out, carrying boxes and issuing instructions to the workmen who arrive with a van, his father simply lies on the sofa with his leg up.

"The doctor said you should do nothing!" she snaps at him, as he tries to pack a vase, inexpertly wrapped in newspaper.

The son blames his father for getting in the way, for not doing as he is told. At the same time, he also blames him for not helping, for being ill and for leaving all of this to his mother.

On the day they move, the cat goes missing. The whole

family looks for her, among the piles of disappearing boxes and in rooms empty but for balls of dust and hair.

He and his sister do not want to leave without her. When the neighbor calls round, they sit on the stairs, unable to make out the words he exchanges with their parents in the kitchen. Afterward, they are told the cat has been found run over in the road outside. His mother steps aside to reveal the cat lying in a cardboard box, a trickle of blood dried at her nose. When he puts his hand under her belly it does not give as normal but remains firm, like the figures they make out of plaster of Paris. Her fur is still soft, but no longer warm. He asks whether they can take her with them, but his mother says no, they must bury her here.

As it grows dark, they climb into the car to make the journey out of town. He watches their home disappear in the rear window, between the slow arcs of the wiper blade. Can they go back and visit the cat? he asks. His parents assure them both that they can but, even then, he knows this to be a lie. They won't go back; they won't visit her. They will only go to school and the school is no longer theirs.

Chapter 4

Their new home is large and drafty in a flat, low-lying village. In the week they move, the lower fields and roads are all submerged by floodwater, with just the tops of hedges and the occasional tree suggesting the landscape hidden beneath. He finds the village cold and damp—its only color variations of muddy brown, against polished white sky.

Now he is recovered, his father sets to work on the land. He claims he always wanted to be a farmer. However, the boy can see this for what it is: they have been thrown out of the town and now his father pretends this is what he wanted all along. His father's leg is no longer swollen and the boy can't help feeling he only played at being ill. Now all he is doing is playing. Playing at anything is embarrassing, but when it is his father—a full-grown man whom everyone used to look up to—it is a humiliation. He would respect his father more were he to hang his head in shame.

While his parents call it a farm, it turns out they only have three fields, all an acre each. His father fences off the first of these, the paddock, with a series of poultry-runs. It is no surprise to him that his father is not good at putting up fences—the posts are never properly set, the wire mesh curls at the bottom like the browned pages of a book. As a result, the hens get out under these gaps and roam into the neighbors' fields and gardens, into the two other fields where they intend to keep sheep. His father is always going round to apologize, inexpertly herding back their flapping bodies with a great stick he thwacks on the ground.

His parents buy a china egg, which they deposit in the central nesting box of the henhouse. One bantam, a white Silkie with feathery boots, goes broody and sits on the egg. Each morning, he and his sister will go outside and laugh at the stupid hen trying to hatch the china egg.

After four weeks, his mother announces it is cruel—the poor bird is wasting her life. He does not feel this way—in some way, he feels the hen deserves it.

Their next-door neighbor, Sidney, disapproves of them being so sentimental. He advises them to douse any broodies with water to get them back to laying. So later that day, with his father standing by the tap, the boy opens the lid and surprises her with the hose. She runs from the nest into the paddock, flapping wet wings.

Sidney is unlike any man the boy has met before. His face is red and round, on top of which sits a flat cap that he fidgets up and down over his forehead. His eyes are shifty, as though anticipating some accusation. In his left hand he carries a stick that breaks into a "Y" at the top, where he rests his thumb. He laughs with a clicking sound.

His mother and Sidney get on, he suspects because she mirrors his voice and intonation when they speak, while his father will not. When she hears Sidney calling over the field, she will pull on her wellies and head out to meet him, resting her foot on the stile and slapping her thigh while they talk across the fence.

Yet, Sidney is easily offended. When he learns that the father has been at the pub questioning his advice on livestock, he challenges the mother, who then comes into the kitchen and curses their neighbor as an overgrown child. A few days pass before Sidney returns to lean over the fence as though nothing has happened.

He makes the family gifts of homemade cider, which they leave untouched in the kitchen, and golden pheasant eggs to hatch under one of the broody hens. When the boy asks where the eggs have come from, Sidney taps his nose. Later his father tells him they have been poached, but far from this bothering his parents, his mother simply slaps her thigh again and they all go on as before. The boy does not think this an adult way to carry on.

It is Sidney who sells them the sheep and offers to

help during lambing season. However, the first lambs all die. The boy looks at their small, rectangular bodies, still warm, buried among the straw. He cannot understand the apparent indifference of the mothers.

Eventually, the vet diagnoses the problem—an infection has poisoned the ewes' milk. They are forced to buy in vast quantities of milk and bottle-feed the lambs. He sits outside the barn door sobbing into his knees at the pitiful noise the lambs make as they are separated from their mothers.

Sidney feels responsible and makes the children a gift of a white-faced lamb, which they bring into the kitchen. Each night the boy and his sister sit by the range, she bottle-feeding it while he reads to it from his copy of *Alice's Adventures in Wonderland*. His parents share this with the men at the pub and he sees how they look, how they set their jaws against him.

The village pub has a tangy smell—of vinegar and the batter of scampi and chips. There is a small pantry that sells crisps, sweets, and ice creams, although they never buy sweets there as the selection is smaller than at the post office in the neighboring village.

The ice creams are in a large freezer, emblazoned with the Wall's logo, with two sliding lids that push out of the way before you can reach the bounty inside. Any child who takes too long choosing will get told off by the landlord for not hurrying their selection and allowing the cold air to escape. The boy has learned not to buy

Calippos, as these melt and shoot out of their cardboard tubes like a fish from a fist.

The men at the pub are different from his father's friends in town. They are farmers and farm laborers who talk in grunts from the dark corners of the bar, where they sit or perch. However, the one thing they have in common with the men in the town is their dislike of women and children. When he and his sister accompany their father, they sit at a distance, while he will stand at the bar.

The boy does not like the men at the pub. They glower at him and fall silent when he is near. Every now and then they will make rough jokes about his mother—about her not liking their drinking, calling to check up on his father, to ask when he will be home. To his horror, sometimes his father will join in. He will come to the pub telephone and say he is leaving immediately, only to order another round. Then he will return to the bar and the watching drinkers, who will laugh and raise their glasses.

The boy has a sense that their roughness extends to him. It is clear he is on his mother's side—on the side of what's right and of manners—and somehow this makes him soft. They laugh and look at him without speaking, waiting for him to leave.

He reckons these men also dislike him because he is only a child. If he sits in the corner reading a book, they will scowl at him. Sometimes they will ask what he is doing, not out of interest but as though he is misbehaving. He may only be a child, their looks say, but they resent his feeling superior to them. The truth is that he does. He does not like their hardness, their drinking, their want of propriety. Worst of all, in hating reading, he feels these men have revealed themselves to be stupid. And yet, his cleverness counts for nothing with them. They are tough, he is soft. This is true because he has allied not only with his mother but also with the life of the mind.

As a result, his preferred visits are those that include his mother, when the whole family is together. He believes they are happiest when all at the pub, when he and his sister can run in the garden or play the arcade machines, when they can ignore the men at the bar.

In the heat of summer, they sit on one of the picnic benches in the beer garden, which banks down to the water's edge. The other diners are all families, visitors from town or day-trippers from Birmingham. He does not like the other children who curse and run between the tables.

They all know what they will have—because it is the same every time they come: his father and sister always order scampi and chips with extra tartar sauce, while he has "Basket Chicken," although the basket is white plastic with a mock weave. Only their mother changes her choice each time, a sign, he believes, of her superior upbringing, her more worldly nature. Sometimes she will have the special, other times the soup of the day. If she is drinking, she will have Dubonnet and bitter lemon, like the Queen Mother; otherwise, she will ask for "a Henry." He is embarrassed at how absurd it sounds.

"It's orange juice and lemonade," she explains to the barman. Then she will turn to them and say, "It's what everyone calls it locally. Everyone calls it 'a Henry.'"

But he feels if this were true, then his mother wouldn't need to explain it every time.

A great yellow Labrador staggers among the tables; a tag around its neck reads, "Please don't feed me. Your kindness is killing me." He does not understand how kindness can kill but, at the same time, he never gives the dog more than one of his chips.

His chicken's caramel-brown skin has the slick lacquer of varnished wood. Wasps hang in the air about the tables, people patting them from their food, back and forth like shuttlecocks. One alights on the lip of his lemonade glass. He looks over at his sister, strands of hair in her Fanta can, and then between his mother and father, smiling with forks in hand, and finally out, across the river, where the sun dances on the surface and a fish lazily flops in the water. Surely no one is as rich as he.

Chapter 5

His father is not good at taking advice. He asks for it, it seems, as a means of disregarding it. Having set his mind on a cow, he ignores all the advice until he can find a farmer willing to sell him one.

"What do you want cows for?" asks one of the men at the pub. "Think of all the trouble you've had with sheep."

On his way to the toilet, the son overhears the same man saying he wouldn't second-guess how the father teaches in school, so why doesn't he listen to their advice on livestock?

In the car home, the son will tell his father that he should listen to the men at the pub. Why does he seek their advice if he will not heed it? By taking their side, he reckons he has set himself against his father and with the men, their arms muscled and brown.

His father buys a cow. A farmer, who they've not met before, brings her over from one of the neighboring villages. This man has a way of speaking that includes a cough and a spit with each sentence, and the son watches the small patches of phlegm dissolve and dry on the ground. He knows that his parents will comment on this later. His father takes a wad of notes from his back pocket, unfolds them and counts them out before putting them into the other man's hand. The man hawks a great sniff through his nose as he counts the bundle again before putting it in his breast pocket.

"And have a pint on me," says his father, pushing another, smaller note into his hand.

"I don't drink," the man coughs. "But thanks," and he raises the note in the air as though making a toast.

"The men at the pub say we shouldn't have a cow," the boy says.

The farmer blinks without speaking.

"They say we wouldn't know what to do with a cow."

His father mutters something and the farmer joins in.

"Looks like your dad would know well enough. Cows aren't difficult." He turns to the father. "Not like sheep."

"The men at the pub say cows are harder than sheep."

"Cows ain't as dumb as sheep."

"No, but they're bigger," says the boy. "And more trouble."

The farmer clears his throat and rocks back on his heels before turning to his truck.

Sure enough, after a few days the cow breaks out of

the paddock. His parents drive around the village in search of her and are then forced to call the local farmers to ask them if they've seen her. After another couple of hours, they call again and ask whether they can help find her. That his father is too old—old or decrepit—to search for his own cow shames the boy.

"I'm so sorry, this is awfully embarrassing," his father says. "Only if you have nothing else to do."

That evening at the pub the men at the bar laugh and signal to one another. His father is an incompetent farmer, that's what their looks say.

"You told him not to buy the cow," the boy says. "I said that when the man brought it. I said you told us not to buy the cow because cows are more trouble than sheep."

He hopes that his stance will curry him favor with these men who talk in grunts and gruffs. By taking their part he is showing he is a man of the world in a way that his father is not.

One man, Gillespie, small and slight who has retired early after injuring his back, gestures with his pipe to his father. "You see! He's heard us well enough."

He feels elevated at this, even when it is so obviously at his father's expense. Or perhaps because of it.

"And they had to go all over the village, all afternoon. And we told him not to get a cow."

The faces at the bar become stern and drop to their drinks. In the silence that follows, it is clear he has not found their favor—he has gone too far. Their common sense includes an expectation of respect due from son to father. By publicly siding against his father, he is breaking a bigger rule he does not understand and somehow placed himself at an even greater remove from them.

"He's going to be Prime Minister one of these days, aren't you?" his father says. "I mean, I've never won an argument with him."

This does not gratify him. He can see that, while these men think a boy has no business arguing with his father, they may also see that to win an argument against his father is no very big thing. Gillespie coughs and juts his lower teeth out as he raises the pint to his lips. And that is it, that is the only response. Somehow, however inadequate his father is in the world of men, he is somehow worse.

Now they have the farm, he sits with his mother in the kitchen of an evening. It's getting dark, even though he's only just home from school. Her face is flushed from bringing logs in from outside and he recognizes that look: the glow is not merely from exerting herself but one of happiness whenever she has a part to play. Now she has thrown herself into the part of a farmer's wife.

She presses her hands against her trousers when she looks at him.

"Why don't you go outside? Why don't you help your father get the cow in?"

She asks him this every day. What he won't say—can't

say—is that he doesn't want to help get the cow in because he's scared of the cow. Cows are big and lumbering and yet at any moment given to spontaneous action. They jump and kick about and he can feel their great, warm bodies pressing in on him. The sheep he doesn't mind; the lambs he picks up and carries in his arms.

So he tells her no, he will stay inside and read his books and she nods approvingly while he feels a guilt at his father out in the fields, waiting for him. In his way, his father will also approve of him spending time with the books, but he knows that this sets them apart.

His sister is like their father. She is able to get on with things. His sister has no fear of the cow. She can anticipate its movements and, when she does, she will bring the large stick down onto the road or the hard ground and, in so doing, indicate the line that she has drawn. It will not cross this line. In this, as in other things, his sister has set down her markers.

While he can always be needled, be forced by their parents to give way—to lend her his books or to allow her into his play—when his sister refuses, she will become as resolute and immovable as the giant mahogany wardrobe on the landing.

He is like their mother. When their mother is not crying or throwing the china on the kitchen floor, she is telling people how happy she is. She will tell them she has never been happier, she has never enjoyed herself so much, never had such a good meal. When she is not profoundly miserable, it seems his mother is always ecstatic. What he knows, and the cow appears to know, is that he has no markers. There is no line that he has drawn that cannot be breached. That is why it gambols near him and will break between him and the line of the hedge. In these moments his father and the workmen will scold him.

Why did he not stop her? Could he not see she was about to break through?

What he cannot say is that he feared he would get hurt, be trampled underfoot. Even cows have the measure of him.

He wishes they grew crops. He could manage that. The planting of a seed and its patient cultivation is something he knows he could manage. There is something nurturing about crops that mirrors the way he treated the lamb penned in on the hearth.

He finds himself saying one day to the collection of stern men at the pub, confiding almost, for it has the solemn weight of a confession, "I think I'd like to be an arable farmer." But as he speaks the men—the laborers, the farmers, the real men—laugh at this, those deep, throaty laughs that knock like wood.

He blushes. He blushes so the roots of his hair flame and they laugh all the more. Yet he dares ask them why. Why are they laughing? Gillespie takes the boy's hands in his own, the man's dark and etched in many pencil lines. And Gillespie doesn't say anything, just turns the child's hands over slowly in his—so that again he becomes ashamed and embarrassed by the gesture. But the man's touch is gentle—the same touch he's seen him use on a runt pup or a chick that needed to be fed and made strong away from its mother. And then he drops the boy's hands without saying anything, turns and swallows his drink; this small, slight man whose spine they said was twisted and curved and growing into itself, like one of those trees with two trunks that twist and grow around itself until it somehow chokes both halves of its being to death. And there is silence in the bar then, as he stands in the middle of the floor, these men, these ashen, weathered men, silent save for the clicking of one of their tongues and the grind as one man sets his jaw forward and coughs. He looks to his father, but his father sits and says nothing.

Chapter 6

Every summer, the day after term finishes, the family packs the car and makes the five-hour journey to Penzance. There, early on Saturday morning, they join a small plane of passengers flying to islands just off the coast. They only come for a week, but it feels longer, and the boy wishes they could stay.

He loves these islands but knows he is just a visitor here. Even though his parents have come since before he was born, and the locals welcome them back every summer, he has an awareness that this place will never be his, that they do not truly belong. He wishes there were some means for him to lay a claim on these islands, in the same way he feels them to claim him. But there is not—they remain outsiders.

His parents become quite different here too: his father wears great canvas shorts, which reveal skinny legs mapped with varicose veins; while his mother goes everywhere with a scarf wrapped around her head to keep her hair from flying about. The only concession to their other life is his father's repeated question: I wonder what's in the post at home. If only they lived here, the boy thinks, then they might be free.

The cottage where they stay is called "Nurses," with whitewashed walls and agapanthus flowers that stand high above the road. He is woken at night by fist-sized raindrops beating against the windows, yet in the morning it is hot and sunny; only the ink-black evergreens and smell of bracken and still-wet grass signal the earlier storm.

When the whole family is awake, they take the path round the heliport and then down along the road, past the Abbey Gardens. From all around comes the loud croak of pheasants.

In the center of the island stands a tiny church. Years ago, his father knitted a kneeler to go in one of the pews and they return to see if it is still there. The church is the one place that feels familiar, with its font, wooden pews, even the green *English Hymnal*—everything here is just the same as it is at home. The only difference is the churchyard, where the ground is sandy and instead of grass it's covered by a lawn of thicker, pricklier leaves. Meanwhile the headstones bear the names of just five families, generation upon generation all with variations of the same names.

They eat in the garden, at a picnic table covered with

a checked tablecloth. Their father roasts a chicken while their mother does a salad, using a colander as an improvised salad bowl. Toward the end of the week, she makes summer pudding from leftover fruit and stale bread. It's too early for blackberries so instead she adds blueberries to the mix of raspberries and strawberries. When she serves it, from a great china basin, the bread is soft and has taken on the deep color of a bruise. It springs apart at the press of her knife.

He takes a book and lies in an old rope hammock, hung between two trees. But he does not read, for he prefers looking up at the sky, at the leaves on the trees that ripple before his eyes like shoals of fish.

In the afternoon, they go down to the beach, next to the quay, where the sand is as soft and powdery as light brown sugar and the chatter of halyards plays against the masts of sailing dinghies, lined up on the shore.

Their mother kneels on the ground and pulls great armfuls of sand toward her. She fashions a keep and ramparts for them, smoothing out walkways and carving steps and battlements, before surrounding it all with a wall, pressed together between the palms of her hands. Finally, she digs a moat with a bridge across, which the children fill with seawater collected in buckets. All the while, a sailing boat topples on a wave in the distance and the sea blurs into the sky.

Later their parents sit up on the breakwater, sketching with tin trays of watercolor paints, while the children scramble over the rocks. The boy's sister lowers her bucket into a rock pool. From some way off, a kite rises.

The boy runs down to the water's edge, where the sea roars upon the beach. He paces the length of the shore, teasing the waves to suck great prints from beneath his feet. But when he turns to retrace his steps, there is now another figure here—a boy about his age.

This other boy dances down the rocks and lands on the sand beneath with a silent thud. His skin is a deep rich color so the watching boy reckons he might be foreign, Italian maybe. As he runs, his shorts sigh away from his hips and the sun catches his thick, dark curls, which shine the color of polished bronze. In one hand he carries a small fishing net, the kind for sale at the gift shop on the quay. As the Italian boy looks up and sees him—sees him but does not wave—he thinks how breathlessly happy he looks, entire to himself.

There's a long pause during which the wind gets up. A sail cracks nearby as an old man hauls a boat and launching trolley down the sand.

The Italian boy runs to his family. They are bright and happy, this rival family; they laugh and joke, the father looks down from his newspaper to tousle his son's hair. This boy and his sister play happily together.

How much kinder, he thinks, he could be to his own sister.

His mother calls him, he needs sun cream, and she pours some into her hand and begins to rub it onto his bare shoulder. But no, he says, he does not want it, does not need it. It has grown cold. He does not want her; he does not want this other boy to see her fussing him.

How horrible he is, how horrible he finds his own family when set against this boy's.

Back home, there is a photo he cherishes from early childhood of him being hoisted onto his father's shoulders, a grin spread across his face. He recognizes the location as one of the fields behind the back of the school, but he has no recollection of it being taken or what he was doing. What is he smiling at? What is he in anticipation of, or has he received, that should elicit such pure joy? But *that*, he likes to think, is how he truly looks. *That* is who he really is. But what happened to that boy? he wonders. Where is he now?

Chapter 7

The new school year starts, cold and fresh. His mother has sat up late into the evening, stitching in name tapes. He had wanted a new uniform but, while his sister received a new skirt, his mother merely let down the hem of his trousers. The only thing that alleviates the awful inevitability of going back, promised by the "Back to School" promotions, which appeared in Smith's as early as July, are his crisp new stationery purchases: a bright new pencil case, devoid of the hole caused by his pair of compasses; a new shatterproof ruler and plastic protractor; a shiny new fountain pen; and bright, sharpened pencils of uniform length.

When it comes to timetabling, older boys judged to have a particular aptitude for art are given extra lessons by Mr. Miller, the English and art master. Mr. Miller is tall, with a Roman nose and dark, heavy hair that stands proud at the back. Like all the masters, he wears a thick jacket made of tweed. Yet, while Mr. Miller's jackets are boxy, with large shoulders, they still hang on him correctly, unlike his father's, which always seem to twist around his body and hang unevenly on either side, as though someone has dressed him from behind.

He would like to grow up to be like Mr. Miller. Compared with the other teachers in the school, he is young and exciting; although, in truth, he is probably no younger than any of them.

While the boy loves English, he is less proficient at art. The harder he tries, the less good his work seems to be. His classmates, the ones who don't care, the ones who fool around on the page, who use the wrong color—red instead of blue for sky, say—those who don't try and make an exact copy of what they see, as he does, are the ones who seem to excel. If he has discerned any secret to what makes good art, then it would seem to be the very act of *not* trying. For this reason, he mistrusts art as a discipline. If the conscientious are to be damned, and the lazy the ones to excel, then what does that say about it as a subject?

Lessons take place in the basement, the bowels of the school, off which is housed a giant boiler that sighs and groans behind a heavy fire door. It is made up of two rooms, the smaller of which is reserved for clay, while the main art room is large and filled with light from a former coalhole, now a fire escape, with a short ladder leading to a large window above their heads.

If there is a rhyme or reason to those selected for extra art, he cannot discern it. It is Mr. Miller himself who selects his protégés, and these boys will be allowed off games, once or twice a week, to build up a portfolio of work.

Mr. Miller only makes protégés of the older boys. If you are in the younger years, Mr. Miller will not befriend nor mentor you. If you are a girl, he will not befriend you either. The only thing these favorites have in common is that they have been chosen.

It seems to have little to do with art, so much as a certain quality that the teacher has perceived in each of them. However, the boy cannot fathom what this quality should be.

When he is selected, the boy reasons this attention at least confirms there is something special about him. And perhaps that is it: Is Mr. Miller capable of distinguishing him from the others owing to some mark of distinction? Is the one thing that these boys, seemingly so different, have in common that each of them, in their own way, is a child prodigy?

He has felt something inside him, something that marks him out as different, but maybe this difference is actually a form of brilliance. Perhaps what has been recognized in him is his artistic genius.

That he is to go on to great things is clear to his parents. Waiting outside the red doors, after school, he hears his father discussing him with the headmaster inside. The word he hears repeatedly is "precocious," a word he does not know, but finds easily enough in the dictionary, kept on top of the toilet at home: "(usually a child) of an advanced intelligence or development for their age."

While he doesn't wish to boast, he feels it important to share this honor, just as one would the captaincy of the under-13 football team or making it into the school choir.

However, his parents do not seem pleased.

His mother cautions him, "I'm not sure it's wholly nice, Daniel. It can be a little derogatory."

He cannot see this himself; the word is used of Mozart. Why should this embarrass his parents? His sister captains all the girls' sports teams, she plays in the orchestra. Why is it only his talent that should be hidden away, not spoken of to spare the feelings of others? Is his greatness to be a burden to him? Would his parents rather he was ordinary?

He has read that great composers, like Chopin and Mozart, began working at a very young age. Mozart composed his first piece at four, a third of his age. That he has not must be down to his laziness.

He has tried composing. A couple of years before, he

wrote an oratorio on sheets of paper that he ruled himself, into five-line staves. He wrote evenings and weekends. He titled it *Wasser*, with an idea of the music tripping and falling like water through the air above his head, and because child prodigies compose in German. Yet when his father played it on the piano it was gibberish. He had had no idea whether the marks, the notations, he had committed to paper bore any relation to the sounds he heard in his head, he only believed they must. Instead of the multiple lines he had imagined—some in harmony, some working against one another—there was only a single line, one note at a time, hammered out in plodding banality.

How did Mozart manage it? How is anyone to do anything if the gap between an idea and its realization, a thought and its expression, should be a chasm? What had happened to the music he heard, the music that drifted above his ahead?

If he is to be great, then clearly it is not in the sphere of music. Indeed, while his parents and others discuss his future greatness, no one will say in what arena this eminence will reveal itself. So how is he to apply himself? How is he to fulfill his destiny without a sign?

Mr. Miller's choosing him is a sign. It marks him out and tells him the path he is meant to take.

He would like Mr. Miller to be his father. Mr. Miller is like the other children's fathers. While his own father is only interested in choirs and pubs, Mr. Miller is interested in books and plays and cricket.

When they work, Mr. Miller will take off his heavy tweed jacket and hang it up on the back of the cupboard door, a repurposed wardrobe that contains all the new paints, charcoals, and inks. These he reserves for the "real" artists—those who spend time with him one on one—while the others are left to poster paints and primary colors out of bottles. The boy appreciates this demarcation, that in this sphere his eminence has been acknowledged.

Mr. Miller rolls up his sleeves, takes a giant sheet of paper and makes great sweeps across it in arcs of color. Then he stands back and asks him to do the same.

He loads a brush and drags it across the cartridge paper, but he is unsure so the line is hesitant like a guttering flame. Even so, Mr. Miller stands back and exclaims, "The boy's a genius," to which he grins from ear to ear, the world's lightness all aglow. Do the stars that burn brightest do so because they have been elevated by Mr. Miller's admiration alone?

Another time, he asks, "How's that?," and the teacher stands back, raises a finger, and exclaims: "Not out, Peter Pan!"

The words reach him bright and clear as the note of a bell.

"I like Peter Pan."

"Of course!"

And this is their pattern: the boy will work studiously at the table, before standing back.

"Howzat?" he will shout, and Mr. Miller will reply, "Not out!," before proclaiming, "The boy's a genius!"

He will make him a gift of his pictures and the man will praise him for it.

Chapter 8

He knows he is a sickly child. This is a fact about himself he resents but cannot change. To be sickly makes him like the namby-pamby mummy's boys in books, the boys that others take the mick out of and will not play with. He would like to be Dickon in *The Secret Garden*, but deep down he knows that he is Colin. Worse still, Colin is not really ill. Colin is not only a namby-pamby, but he chooses to be so. When the other children take him out, encourage him to walk, he can, he is fine. Colin's illness is only make-believe.

His illnesses are not make-believe. He regularly gets temperatures over a hundred and three. His mother will call out the doctor, who will come grudgingly, only to confirm, on sight of him, that he is, truly, very sick. When he gets these fevers, he knows he is bad when the pattern on his parents' bedspread takes on a life of its own. The dark-green ivy will begin to grow and, as he cuddles up to his mother, his hand above the covers, he will scream as the green tendrils grow up and over his hands.

Yet there are other times when he is not sick, when he wakes up simply with his head full of cold and says he cannot go into school. His mother requires little convincing. She says she would rather he has one day off, to get over something, than miss a whole week of class. This way he will stay home.

His sister will scowl at him, demand to know why she cannot be let off school, to which he will say he is not being let off, he is sick. She will pick up her bag and kick at his feet. "You're not, Danny," she says. "You're faking. You're skiving."

His father is of his sister's party. On days he has gone out first thing in the morning, he will return to find his son, dressed in just pajamas, curled up on the sofa watching cartoons.

"Why are you at home?" he asks.

"I'm ill."

His father says nothing to this, which is more damning than if he were to argue.

Later he learns that his attendance record is the worst in the school. Of all the possible schooldays, he has attended only sixty percent. Mr. Miller calls him a skiver—says it is ridiculous he should be allowed to miss so much—while his form master tells him that school is very important. It is important for him not to miss days. He must try to come in. He nods.

However, what he wants to say is that he would have come in if he could, but he has been, truly, very sick. By impressing on him the importance of his coming to school, the form master makes it clear that, like his father and sister, he also does not believe the notes written for him by his mother, nor the excuses he gives his classmates.

Yet, in spite of all these absences, he still comes top of the class. Therefore, he deduces that school is not important to him getting good marks—he can manage perfectly well at home. There is nothing he can miss that he cannot make up. This only confirms his intuition that school is pointless. Or that the point of school is not to learn, that if school has a point then it is a secret one, one not to be shared with the children.

What he cannot say, cannot admit, is that there are occasions when he is off school simply because he is exhausted. The boredom of science classes that teach him things he cannot ever imagine finding useful, the anxiety over what it is he is to say in interactions with classmates when he knows nothing of football, the small ways he seems to annoy them even as he tries to make them like him, all these things tire him out. He would much rather be at home. At home he can read his books. In between, he can watch cartoons on the TV.

Sometimes his father will buy him magazines from Smiths, partworks about famous composers, artists, or writers. He likes these best as they come with a cassette or book and he has the idea of, bit by bit, building up a collection, a library of his own. While his father buys him magazines, his mother will come and sit with him, talk to him. He would much rather spend time with his mother than the rough children at school.

However, every time he returns to school he senses he has lost something. As much as he wishes he need never go to school, and is grateful to his mother for letting him off, he also blames her for indulging him quite so readily. Her doing so reduces him in the eyes of his peers. Her letters are responsible for this, her letters and her conversations with the teachers. If only she could be more effusive, more detailed in her descriptions of the times he is gravely ill, he feels sure everyone at school would understand the parlous state he is in. That they do not must, in some ways, be down to her.

Then again, his father makes no attempt at all. His father has regular meetings with the new headmaster. He does not know what these are about, nor if his absences ever come up in conversation. However, he feels sure that were his father asked he would make no attempt to speak for him. His father does not believe he is ill on the days he stays home and watches cartoons, his father does not even seem to worry for him on the evenings when the doctor is called out. In this way, his father cannot care for him at all, and certainly not enough to speak on his behalf. In this, as in all respects, his father takes the other side; he will always take the side against him.

ᕳᕲ

A new boy has joined his class. Their first lesson is games. He does not welcome new additions—they disturb the carefully tuned balance, the hierarchy established over time. In truth, he must concede that this is a hierarchy in which he holds a lowly status. He is not good at games, he is not good at sport generally, he is not well liked by the other children for being a sickly mummy's boy. Even though he gets the top marks, this does not seem to confer any social benefit upon him.

This new boy is taller than him, with fair, curly hair, and limbs that are tanned from a life lived outside. His own skin is pale—bleached white—and his arms and legs skinny and undeveloped. If he had a body like this boy's, then he too would strip off with confidence, he too would spend hours outdoors, playing cricket or football. The sun would also shine on him.

He studies this boy's rangy movements, the way his shorts cling to his buttocks and thighs, the gather of the fabric between his legs, the hollow his collar makes when he leans forward to talk, the way he props himself up on a chair. He would like to move like this boy. He moves without hesitation or fear, as though the world belongs to him.

He reckons Philip, for that is the new boy's name, is shy. He sits by himself, always at some remove; he arrives late to every class and hangs back at break, so he grows curious about him. What thoughts keep him company, alone at his desk? How is it he is sufficient to himself?

Over time, he reasons that by judiciously choosing his seat, he might find himself sat next to Philip when Philip duly arrives late to class. But as hard as he tries, he finds no rhyme or reason to this new boy's selection of a seat. Until he realizes that if he arrived even later he could choose the seat next to him, the one Philip has chosen precisely because he prefers to sit alone and the pair of seats are vacant.

He contrives a reason to be detained in the cloak-room, waiting as long as he dares, before showing up late to class, apologizing to the teacher and selecting, of the only two remaining seats, the one next to this boy who fascinates him. He sits and gives an awkward smile, to which Philip smiles also.

Philip also excels in class. Now, when the marks are handed out, it is a toss-up as to which of the two of them will have come top. Worse still, following any of his periods of absence, he will return to find Philip has assailed all the tests, tests that he must now make up in his own time. To be ill means to concede any advantage to Philip.

He wonders whether Philip is his nemesis. All people of significance have a nemesis: Sherlock Holmes and Moriarty, Rudolf Rassendyll and Rupert of Hentzau, Richard Hannay and the man with the hooded eyes. Perhaps Philip is his. Or is it simply that Philip will supplant him in his own story? He can think of nothing more humiliating than failing to be the hero of one's own story, just as his father has failed to be the man of the house. All the same, he must concede to a pang of intuition—that this boy matters, somehow, in a way that he does not.

This boy, with his glorious body, will be normal. He will grow tall, his voice will drop. He will play sports, and run through fields, climb trees and stretch his limbs. Later he will know how to talk with girls, how to move next to them. He has a knowledge that is deep and cannot be taught.

The boy understands injustice, that fate makes gifts to some and not others. Yet the fact that while the world worries him, and he worries the world, there are others who are never bothered in this way at all, seems to him of a different order. There are people in life, he recognizes, who have been blessed. They have a way of being— a way of moving in the world—something he cannot describe. But they have been chosen, or born with a facility denied to others.

Or is it the other way round? Maybe it is not that he lacks something, so much as he knows something he should not? Does he hold a knowledge, a gift or inheritance, he cannot shake off? Either way, this strikes him as deeply unfair.

In this way, this other boy is his impossible self. He awakens something in him with the relentless strike of piano keys. He would like to be this boy. Or to have something of his. If he could be someone else, then he would be this boy. This is the boy he is meant to be.

Chapter 9

Over half term he goes out shopping with his mother. He would rather they were in Cheltenham, where the shops are bigger, grander and more numerous, where there are cinemas and an arcade. The avenues and promenade in Cheltenham will be full now of fallen leaves, helter-skeltering above the pavements and banking up in shop doorways. People will be smartly dressed, in coats, hats and gloves, along with a phalanx of umbrellas.

Philip tells him they go to Cheltenham every weekend. If only they went to Cheltenham, he feels sure they'd bump into Philip, they might even be allowed to get colas and a bun.

His mother, however, hates driving into Cheltenham: it is too far, too busy, and she finds it too difficult to park. So instead, they walk up from the bank, past the meager smattering of shops on Barton Street, before pausing outside a dress shop. He complains of being bored but his mother tells him that, for her, dresses are like books.

In the window is a long, red dress made of a delicate material that falls soft and slow as light through an open window. He can tell it is very beautiful.

"Do you mind if we go in?" she asks.

He tells her it is fine.

The woman in the shop asks his mother if she would like to try it on.

"I don't know if my husband would like it," she says, turning in front of the mirror and pressing her hands the length of the fabric. "He doesn't approve of backless dresses."

The woman pulls a face.

"Or red."

The woman's face draws him into some kind of secret. He does not like that this strange woman should conspire against his father. On the other hand, he can't fail to acknowledge his mother looks very beautiful in the dress. He resolves that his mother should have the red dress.

Out in the street, he asks, "Would he really not let you have it?"

"Oh no, I'm sure he wouldn't mind," she tells him. "His age just means he's a little old-fashioned in his tastes, that's all."

"Then why did you say it?"

"Oh, it's just what one says, isn't it? One must have some excuse," his mother tells him.

He does not understand why his mother would lie merely to draw in the woman at the dress shop. But nor can he understand why his father would not like backless dresses, or red ones. He does not like red as much as blue, but it is still a perfectly good color.

Ultimately, he agrees his father's age spoils many things. If his father were younger, he wouldn't stop to grab the arthritis in his knee as they walk down the high street; he wouldn't need a hand to get out of a boat on holiday; he would be able to chase them in the park; he would be able to play cricket out on the lawn.

His mother is something of a beauty, everyone says so. And therefore, it surprises him that she should have married his father. His father behaves like a man who cannot believe his luck. To the men at the pub, he says he cannot understand why such a beautiful woman ever married a man as fat and old as he is.

He wishes his father had more self-respect. If his father is so unworthy of his mother, then he should have done the decent thing and never married her at all.

Originally, she had trained to be an actress, before her parents forced her to enroll at teacher training college. Being an actress, she tells him, was not regarded as a proper profession.

He can tell that his mother would have been a great actress owing to her ability to become whomever she is talking to. However, he must admit, when she does this, she has a tendency to gush. If she is talking to a workman she'll speak from the back of her throat and become rough, even a little coarse; if she speaks to one of the fine old ladies in church on Sunday, she will emphasize her vowels and play with the silk scarf about her neck; when she talks to Sidney she slaps her thigh and says "ooh-aah" like one of the pirates in *Swiss Family Robinson.* Overacting is the one constant in her performances, and it makes him sad she is not better at it.

Sometimes, when they watch television as a family, she'll point to someone on screen whom she trained with. "He used to be so good-looking," she'll say. Or, "She had to bare her breasts on stage."

You can still be an actress, he tells her. It is important to him that she not give up on what she calls "the stage." It is important to him that she lives her true life, that she be the great actress he knows her to be.

To him it is simple: everyone has a true life, a true self, they are destined to fulfill. If she wants to act, she should act. For her to have given up on acting makes him unaccountably sad, as though she has given up on life itself. He wishes she had never told him about it—what if she was not good enough at acting to live the life she was meant to live?

Or worse, what if her true life is one without him at all?

The only thing that can have changed is her marriage to his father. His father had the school and now the farm. It is only his mother who is not allowed to do as she wants. She must be a wife and then the mother of his children and, in doing so, she can no longer act. This strikes him as typical. His father, who does not like her to wear red, or a backless dress, is preventing her from being a star on stage or screen. If his father were less selfish then his mother could be happy. She could be herself. He knows by listening to her, the way she tells stories, the faces and gestures she makes, she would be a very great actress. She is more beautiful than other mothers so he can well believe she is more beautiful than the women in films, the films she refuses to take him and his sister to see. He presumes this is why his father does not want her to act, it will reveal to the world what is evident to the son, that he has no business being married to this woman who is so much better than he is.

As they continue their shopping, she tells him the story of *Romeo and Juliet*. He knows of William Shakespeare, he has seen the dusty, leather-bound edition with gold edging his parents have on the bookcase. While he can't make out much from the words, he senses he would like to be this man, this man whose work resides in a volume resembling a magician's spell book. As they walk down the high street his mother tells him about the two families at war with one another, terrorizing the city.

"Like this one?" he asks.

"A bit," she says. "Although this is more of a town. Bigger than this one."

"Why do they hate each other?" he asks.

"I don't know. Sometimes people just fall out. Think

of the Masons and the Dudleys. They haven't spoken for fifty years."

As his mother speaks, he decides he would be a Montague—he prefers the sound of the word and the shape it makes in his mouth. She tells him about the children of these families, the ball at which they meet and how they fall in love. She tells him of Romeo's best friend, the playful, charismatic Mercutio, and Juliet's jealous, possessive cousin. He can tell from the way she speaks how much his mother dislikes, disapproves of Tybalt.

Midway up the high street, rain begins to fall. Water beads off the handles of his mother's shopping bags. The breath stops in his mouth as she tells him how Mercutio is killed—so badly hurt that he's turned into worms' meat—"Like cat food," she explains—and he bounces on the balls of his feet as she describes Romeo avenging his friend's death.

"And what? What then?" he begs.

But by this point they have reached the greengrocers.

"You'll have to wait," she tells him. "I need to pop in for potatoes and carrots. People won't want to hear me telling you stories."

"No," he pleads. "Tell me now. I must know!"

"Stop that," she tells him, entering the grocers so he is forced to wait a few minutes outside.

The rain drips from the awning with the metallic sound of the change he watches being counted into her hand through the cloudy window. Later she will tell him how the story ends, but its force has gone. In fact, he finds it disappointing. Even if she has demonstrated the power of stories, he does not think this one worthy of his anticipation.

꿈

It is two weeks later when his mother starts her fits of crying. It begins one morning, as he and his sister are readying for school. They enter the kitchen to find her hunched over the table in tears, a handkerchief balled up in her hand, sweating against the vinyl tablecloth. They ask what is wrong but she tells them it is nothing. She apologizes but she does not stop, she does not move. They have never seen either of their parents cry before. That morning it is their father who takes them in to school.

He is troubled all day long. His teacher crouches down next to his desk, her skirts flowing over her shoes to the floor. She asks if he's feeling ill. For once, he says no.

"What's wrong then?" she asks. He tells her that his mother has been crying. "Oh, is that all," she says. "I cry all the time."

This does not comfort him. Now, not only does he have his mother's tears to worry about but his teacher's too.

In the evening his mother's face is pale and lined. She does not get supper but retires to her room. When he goes up and hugs her, she hugs him back, but weakly, as though she is withholding something.

Later, he and his sister huddle next to each other on the sofa. They do not bicker, as they usually would, but sit in uneasy silence. He asks about her day and feels protective when she tells him of a girl who said she only got captain of hockey because of their father. He resolves to protect his sister and hurt anyone who hurts her.

Over the following months his mother seems to cry more and more. Her crying is not public, instead she hides away. He and his sister will be busy playing or watching TV and call for her, only to find she does not answer, or will not come. When they go looking for her, they will stumble into her room and find her in bed, her face hidden in the pillows, eyes big, a face that has collapsed to her chin. Or they will hear her through the bedroom door, choking on sobs like a cat with a furball. Then they will stand there, facing each other, their stockinged toes almost touching, waiting for they know not what.

They grow used to standing still, learn where the floorboards creak and move, and grow accustomed, through indecision, to the silent turning of the door handle and its gentle release as they fall back from going inside.

In this, and in many other ways, her crying makes their mother absent. She either disappears from the house for hours at a time, or deep within it. He feels her somehow lost in her crying. What if she leaves? he wonders.

He will climb in next to her, cuddle her. Tell her he

loves her and kiss her. He will do whatever is necessary to make her better, to make her stay. He does not want her to leave. He does not wish for them to be left with just their father. With their father, they'd be all alone.

He cannot think what is upsetting her. He also has an awareness that when his mother is crying it should be his father who comforts her, not him or his sister. But it would seem none of them want to be left on their own in the house with her upstairs.

One day, when he finds her crying in the living room, he calls his father. But his father will not come. Eventually, when he does, it is only to look around the door, ask what is wrong, before awkwardly walking away. After a while, the boy hears the car start and then reverse in the drive. When he walks outside it is to see his father driving off.

His father disappears to the pub earlier and earlier. The pub does not open until seven, but his father always arrives just after six.

He tells his father, "You shouldn't go down until seven. They only open at seven."

"They don't mind," his father says.

"They might. If they wanted to open at six, they'd open at six. They might be busy. They might be having a nap. If they open at seven, then you should only go down at seven."

However, he knows this is not the case because when they go together, his father will try the door and let himself in, walk to the bar and call out for the landlord. If the door is locked, he will knock and tap on the glass with his car keys. To the boy's surprise, the door is always opened to him, they always let him in.

"Oh, okay," his father snaps, "I won't go down until seven."

He knows full well his father does not mean this. Sure enough, the next day his car disappears just after six. Worse still, his father goes without him. If he does not go when his father pleases, then he does not get to go at all.

Chapter 10

Wiping down the worktables, Mr. Miller asks whether he would like a companion during these one-to-one art lessons. Rainbows arc from beneath the master's hand as the water interacts with flecks of paint and colored chalks.

The question suggests a benefit or concession to him. Yet, far from a benefit, the boy feels sharing the teacher would be a loss.

"I think we should ask Philip to join us one of these days," the teacher says. "What do you think?"

He does not know what to say: although he likes Philip very much, Mr. Miller's question does not feel a true question.

"Why would we ask him?"

"Well, he's also very good at art. It would be good to have someone else for you to work with. Maybe even some competition."

There is a pause and Mr. Miller stands up from his work. "He's a very bright boy, isn't he? Very—alive."

The boy does not wish to acknowledge this; something else he does not wish to share, to have meted out between them.

"My marks are better."

"Oh yes, Peter Pan!" Mr. Miller gushes. "He is bright like that, maybe even as bright as you, but I meant more—he *burns* brightly, do you know what I mean?"

He does: there is a glow to Philip that warms him when the two of them are together, which draws him in so he wishes to stay near him for as long as possible. Yet, at the same time, he feels Mr. Miller is making a claim of Philip, one he mightn't make of himself. Why is he not enough on his own?

If Mr. Miller has already made up his mind, then why does he ask for his opinion? Why pretend that Philip's presence should be for his benefit when he doesn't want him to join?

As a result, every Tuesday and Thursday afternoon, he and Philip are together in the art room. Mr. Miller joins them on Thursdays, but on Tuesdays they are left alone. He doesn't know why Philip has agreed to join when Philip likes sport, is in each of the teams and essential to the play. However, he senses that maybe Philip, who is strangely shy with other children, likes the solitude of the art room, likes the quiet companionship of an afternoon, nearly as much as he does.

When they are alone, the art room feels a forgotten realm. Conversation drops through the open window of the fire escape, clear and distinct in the cold winter air. At half past one, trainers and games socks march out to the playing fields, followed by the boom of the games master's voice and the thud of a giant bag of rugby balls. Then all is quiet. Every now and again the main door to the school will go and the secretary's steps trip along the path to the school hall and back.

The pair of them work on different tables in studied silence. He imagines this to be what a job feels like. Previously, he has felt bound to fill a silence, to place himself into it, to remind it of his presence. But with Philip the silence becomes their own, an energetic silence that follows them around, clothes them, drawing them closer. They only stop to speak and comment on one another's work. He likes that Philip asks for his opinion.

In exchange, Philip gets him talking about girls, dates, and whatever older boys do. Philip knows because he has an older brother. He could not have this talk with anyone else—the others are too crass and he fears the words would sound too uncertain or stupid in his mouth. But Philip lets him talk. He tells Philip everything about himself, talks himself out, until there is nothing left to share.

He cannot discern why Philip is friends with him. Philip can be friends with whomever he wants. He'd imagined that their rivalry for the best marks would make Philip despise him, but instead it has brought them together. Somehow there is something in him that Philip likes.

Over the weeks, he finds he has slowly begun aping Philip's gestures and behaviors. When he sits, Philip will absentmindedly throw one arm around the back of the chair, as though pulling it and those around him into a casual embrace. There is something so at ease in this gesture, so confident, he must mimic it. And yet, however he sits, he is too short for his arm to run comfortably along and around the chair, so that his shoulders hunch about his neck. What he displays is merely discomfort.

To be shy and timid is not how he believes himself to be. So when he catches himself sitting like a child with his knees touching at the end of lunch, he studies the older boys to determine how he should behave. They swing their legs over the benches, to face out, waiting to be dismissed, and spread their legs wide apart. Yet, when he imitates them, they grin over and mirror with exaggerated gestures. What is it that gives him away?

It becomes evident that, of the two of them, Philip is the better artist. Philip's being here makes sense in a way that his does not. Never is this clearer than when they set their work side by side and, now, all the master's earlier exclamations are reserved for Philip. He is merely rebuked. He is told that he has not observed a line as well as Philip, that his perspective of the roof is off, that Philip has used bold lines and contrast, while he has fiddled about in one corner.

"Try again," the teacher says.

He makes a mark. The teacher rubs it out.

"Try again."

Again he rubs it out.

"Again."

"Again! Can you not see? Why do you keep drawing a window there?" he says, jabbing the paper.

"Because there is a window there."

"But can you see it? Can you see it in the photo? The shadow makes it the same color as the wall! You can't see a window there. You are not looking, you're guessing!"

What he would like to do is draw himself out in lines, to pour himself out in bright color across the page with abandon. But instead his marks are halting and hesitant, the colors so fussed over that they become dirty and brown.

On some of the days they have tuition, Mr. Miller will grow angry, scratching across his work with the wooden end of the paintbrush. The lines all indicate the various things he has attempted to copy meticulously from life, only to find he has fabricated them: a wall too tall, another too short, perspective angled wrong, an additional window, a figure he has entirely invented.

"You're not concentrating!" Mr. Miller snaps.

He cannot believe this—he can hardly move for concentrating. In this way, Mr. Miller is inconsistent. At times the man flares up.

"You're thinking too much—let your hand go free."

And with this, the teacher will place his larger hand over the boy's and sweep it across the paper. If he interjects to say the boat is not that long, its bow not that deep, Mr. Miller will throw his hands in the air freely and cry, "You think too much, Peter Pan! Don't overthink it!"

Well, which is it? he wants to know. Should he concentrate or not think? How is one to stop thinking, yet still pay attention?

"What would you do?" he asks Philip. "I did him three sketches, I painted one of them up. I don't see what is so different between our drawings."

"I don't know," replies Philip. "Maybe you shade it too much. He keeps telling you not to."

"I don't think that's it. What have you done? What does he tell you that he doesn't tell me?"

"Nothing."

He doesn't want to say these things, only think them, but they tumble from him anyhow. What he really wants to ask is, Why does he always like yours better than mine?

౼

Away from the swagger of the changing rooms, he and Philip can confide to one another. Philip is eating extra greens to encourage his growth spurt. That Philip, who is taller than he is, should be worrying about this as well comes as a welcome surprise. He in turn confesses that, being smaller, he's frightened of getting into a fight with the other boys. He does not know how to fight. He is frightened of pain. Philip says he'll show him what to do. They set their work aside and square up to one another.

"See my fist," Philip says. "See how I wrap my thumb in my fore and middle finger and so they stick out a bit?" And before he can answer Philip punches him on the upper arm. It's not the pain that hits him first but the numbness. The pain comes later.

"It's a dead arm," Philip explains. "That's what you need to do. You don't punch with your knuckles, you use your finger bones."

He doesn't want to complain or moan in front of Philip. He bears it. And bearing it for Philip is easier.

They don't return to their pictures for the rest of the afternoon, but continue to square up to each other, making attempts on one another's arms and legs. If ever either of them gets a good hit in then he stands back and lets the other recover. They also grin. Somehow the pain is good—a fact that pleases them both.

At four o'clock, voices can be heard outside again, and the clatter of studs and shower of dry mud on the steps to the changing rooms. He doesn't want this afternoon to end. Their friendship is not secret, yet outside it has none of the intimacy of these hours. Philip is someone else in the art room and, in this way, the boy feels he is privileged with a glimpse of Philip's true self.

Chapter 11

Although spring is only round the corner, the weather has grown cold. The ground is hard, flecked with frost even in the afternoon. Ice forms and then cracks where water puddles in the old ruts of tractor tires.

He is off school again and when it has been a week, his mother takes him out for a drive. Windows wink as they pass and smoke rises from chimney stacks, so he can almost feel the texture of it, warm and soft as breath blown across the face. She turns up the car heater and says they'll stop somewhere and buy sweets so long as he doesn't tell his sister. He feels this is the closest to when he was little—before he was forced to go to school, before he was forced to share his mother.

They get lost, then more lost, as they turn down side roads they've passed but never taken before and drive around villages they've only known as signposts. He didn't know you could get lost so close to home.

"We can," his mother says, "because we don't need to be anywhere."

He loves her like this.

Later, they find their way home only gradually, stopping at a crossroads to look at a church through the car windows. They slow to a crawl past a grand estate, with a Victorian lodge and gatehouse, brickwork patterned like the top of a crown and finials above the windows. They crane their necks to look up a long driveway to tall windows and long, dark hedges.

"Imagine what it would be like if we lived there," she says, and they both do.

They continue past a white-painted house with a pool outside, its water the bright blue of food coloring. And in each gap between houses there is darkness, and he feels the gap like a held breath before one makes a choice.

"Look at all the lives we could have," she says again. "Imagine. Imagine how happy we would be."

He wants to stay here with her, his feet warm in the footwell, driving around and around, looking at all the lives, the people, the stories they could choose. He doesn't want to have to choose, to grow old, for life's paths to gradually close off, one by one. If only we never need choose; from the warmed air of the car, he could have them all—stay exactly as he is, on the threshold, on the cusp of choice, where everything is possible, where, in that moment, cuddled to his mother, he can have everything. All the stories belong to them.

Usually, when he is off school, he will watch mid-morning television. His sole reason for watching is the phone-ins, with the slow cycle of callers parading their unhappy lives in return for advice.

The hosts of this show, Richard and Judy, are husband and wife. He does not like them. The husband's advice is glib and judgmental: "Just dump him," on suspicions of cheating; "Just kick her out," on a daughter causing havoc at home; "Go to the doctor and get some antidepressants." It is clear this man's advice is not to be taken seriously.

No, the reason he watches is for the psychotherapist, Dr. Raj. Dr. Raj has an air of quiet authority. He reveals these people's problems are not as they appear, that they are altogether something else. They have secret lives, lives they know nothing of.

The woman struggling with her mother-in-law is not really annoyed about who will cook the Sunday lunch, she is in competition with her for her husband. Her husband refuses to grow up, he will not separate from his mother, while the mother is jealous of her—his wife.

By asking his questions, Dr. Raj will discern the truth of the matter—that their past holds a clue to their current predicament.

He admires the way Dr. Raj draws people out, that he can tell them things about themselves they do not know. He is astounded that, with these stories, the psychologist reveals a secret life, one beneath the basic story we tell.

People are just like books—full of hidden meanings that need to be unearthed by an attentive reader. He would also like the secret knowledge held by Dr. Raj.

To have had this realization sets him apart from his parents. His parents believe the surface of their story, they have no knowledge of their real life. This is why his mother is unhappy, while his father is incapable of being the man of the house. If his parents cannot see this, then it is up to him to show them.

Every time they have guests over, his father will disappear to search for a browned press cutting from *The Times*. In it, a man—who looks almost completely unlike his father—is photographed on stage with a group of others in costume. A beautiful, middle-aged woman is the only one seated, in the center of this crowd.

As an undergraduate at Cambridge, his father missed a tutorial to take the stage in London with Joan Sutherland. The boy does not know who Joan Sutherland is, although the name places her among the old women his mother visits. His father's tutor asked if he could get Miss Sutherland's autograph.

It seems tragic to him that his father's greatest boast should be about a time when he was twenty. Why did he not make this the beginning of a life he could boast about, as opposed to living a life in which this is the only boast?

So one day, he finds his father's press cutting, screws it up and hides it deep within the bonfire at the bottom of the garden. He waits for his father to set the whole lot ablaze and stands back admiring the heat while stood next to him. The next time they have guests over his father searches for the cutting but to no avail. The boy is satisfied to have cut his father off from his illusion.

Yet, what he doesn't acknowledge, but can't help feeling, deep down, is that the reason neither of his parents have followed the destiny set out for them is because of him. Rather than the life they could and should have led, they have both chosen a different path, one that has led to him and his sister.

The thought he dares not think, the thought set apart on a railway siding, is what a debt he and his sister owe their parents. When he lies awake at night, the weight of this makes his face grow hot and wet upon the pillow. He is insufficient to the burden of living his own life, let alone one worthy of the lives his parents have sacrificed for him.

And yet, he never asked his parents to incur such a cost, and this merely compounds the debt further, for he is not even grateful to them—hates them for it, in fact. And so he cries himself to sleep, muddled up at his own lack of worthiness for what his parents have done for him, while hating them for having done it at all.

Chapter 12

In the mornings, when their father drives them to school, they pass a line of children walking in gaggles of blue blazers and rucksacks to wait at the bus stop. These are the local children who go to the local school. He does not know why he and his sister do not go to the local school, at least now that their father is no longer headmaster of the prep. However, he knows about the local children, has heard stories of their bad language; that later they will smoke, do drugs, and have sex.

From the safety of the car, he watches them push and shove each other off the pavement. Were he to go to the local school, he knows he would get beaten up. Just as the men at the pub find him odd and suspicious, so too would their sons and daughters. He knows the local children are to be feared.

It doesn't help that his uniform, of salmon-pink jersey and tie, makes him a target for ridicule. One day, when walking through town after school, he sees two local boys approaching him, so he crosses to the other side of the street. Near the war memorial, before the high street, they cross over too. They are the kind of boys his mother has warned him about, boys who walk with their shoulders. They can't be any older than him, indeed they may even be a little younger. But he can feel their presence, pressing up against him. He tries not to look, makes an effort to look the other way.

As they draw level, the taller of the two spits at him, "Ponce!" He cannot think what to say in return. When he glances back, the boy meets his gaze, so he looks away before he will say it again. It's not a word he has heard before. He does not know this word, nor what it means. Yet in some way he does.

When he gets home, he looks it up in the dictionary. He reckons this word cannot apply to himself, that it only applies to adults. However, he fears they may have hit on something. He feels sure they have.

He can't imagine them shouting at Philip, or his sister. Or if they did, the word would not stick to them in the way it does to him now.

Perhaps he is only singled out because he insists on being different. Just as he feels his reading should confer a superiority on him which it does not, so too he feels his going to his father's school should distinguish him, when maybe it only marks him out as in need of protection. Far from being distinguished, perhaps he only goes to his father's school because he is unsafe to walk on his own, because he cannot handle the local children, because he is marked out as in some way strange. In this way, the local children are of the world, while he must be shielded from it.

༄

In a similar way, he gets to wondering whether his family's superiority only masks their oddness. His father votes Conservative. His father dislikes their local MP, but he fears Labour will abolish private education. His mother votes Liberal Democrat. He would like both of his parents to vote Labour. He cannot understand why, when they are always giving people money and helping the poor, neither of them will vote for a party that makes that its duty.

That he supports Labour has become something of a family joke. By supporting Labour, he has set himself against the family, against his father. No one in the village, or down the pub, votes Labour. The men at the pub deride Labour for its lack of feeling toward the country way of life.

As far as he can tell, the country way of life means hunting and fishing. He doesn't agree with hunting or fishing. However, what he doesn't understand is why the men at the pub—men who neither hunt nor fish, men without a farm, the men who are laborers—hate Labour and support hunting.

One day Sidney stops in the pub after a day at the cattle market. He asks if they want to hear a joke and gestures for the boy and his sister to stand in front of him. Then, from the height of his barstool, he asks if they know why some Muslims come to have a spot in the center of their forehead? No, they both tell him, they don't know. Solemnly, Sidney points a finger and taps each of them in the middle of the forehead as he repeats, "You will not have a council home!" He bursts out laughing.

They join in the laughter, their father too. Nearby, Gillespie clears his throat. There is a quality to this joke, something adult that the boy does not fully understand, but its incongruous conclusion amuses him.

When they drive home, they repeat it in the car. At home, they compete to tell it to their mother. The joke is passed between them, their father joins in.

"I'm not sure that's a very nice joke," she says.

He feels this is typical of her. His mother doesn't like anything that sounds critical of anyone or anything, even if it's in the name of humor. But his mother is adamant—it's in poor taste, she says.

The next day, he and his sister try the joke at school. They don't often socialize together, but they want to show their classmates that they too, like normal families, belong to a community. Other children share the crude stories their fathers bring home from work. He wants to have insider jokes, insider stories. He has envied them. Now he hopes they will envy him.

He and his sister stand ringed by classmates. His sister defers to him, lets him do the set-up, allows him to ask the question. But when the time comes, they both say in unison, prodding the brow of the person nearest each of them: You will not have a council home.

No one laughs. No one laughs as they did the other night. Far from an outlier, their mother seems to have sensed the atmosphere of the schoolyard. One boy, a farmer's son, known for risqué and inappropriate jokes, says, "I think that's a bit racist." A girl with plaits says it isn't Muslims who have a mark on their head, it's Sikhs. On the edge of the group, Philip and a few of the boys turn away. He tries to catch Philip's eye but fails and soon there is the sound of a ball pounding against the playground wall.

He wants to defend Sidney but he cannot think what to say, how to make sense of the village, their evenings at the pub, how to make the joke flower anew.

He'd have expected better of his sister: his sister is the most normal, the most socially adjusted of the family. That his mother, who knows no jokes, should understand what is and is not acceptable humor surprises him. It is their father who is always at the pub, always telling jokes, so what has his father not understood? Are they a racist family? Above all, he fears this proves they are not normal. Even next to the families who hate immigrants and gypsies and Europe, he and his family are beyond the pale.

Chapter 13

As the days lengthen the heat grows, and in the fading light of evening bursts of blooms steam in the falling dew. Up in the sky, arrows of black swoop and dive, skimming the ground. He runs from the back of the house to the kitchen, where his parents are, his breath hot with excitement.

"The swallows are back!" he shouts. "The swallows are back!"

They follow him out the door: him running, his mother walking, his father some way behind. They join him to find a line of small, cloaked figures perched on the telephone wire.

When he is sent upstairs to bed, his chest is tight to burst. He throws open his bedroom window to let in the world shut outside—the songs of the birds, the lambs in the fields, the cars driven by teenagers down to the river. How can he possibly sleep, when he is missing everything, locked away? The world is happening outside. He screws up his fists and rests them on the sill, leaning out and looking for the sun in the blushing sky.

"Good night, Mummy," he calls. "Good night, Daddy." And then, making sure not to leave anyone out, he calls good night to each of the animals by name. Finally, he calls, "Good night, God," and reckons that God must hear this, that really all these good nights have been for God.

～

Eight weeks after the birth of this year's lambs, he wakes to the sound of the pickup truck belonging to the farmer up the road. His parents are outside, the sheep all penned in and his father in boots ready for work.

"We only want the males," the farmer says, and the boy looks at his father and looks at the lambs.

The man has a pair of silver scissors, but instead of sharpened blades these have metal prongs on each of their points, over which the farmer places a black rubber ring. His father tells him this is an elastic band, but he sees this is not true, for it is neither brown nor elastic, but small and tight. He stands close by and watches as they sit the lamb on his father's lap, as though sat upright at a table. The farmer opens the scissors ever so slightly and rings the area between the lamb's legs before ringing its tail.

"What happened?" he asks.

"It's so their tails will drop off," the farmer replies.

"How?"

"It stops the blood and it turns black and finally falls off."

He does not ask them about the other ring, the ring between their legs. For weeks following the farmer's visit, he scours the ground of the paddock for the shriveled raisins of what once would have made them rams.

He knows this happens to boys too. In his *Tree of Knowledge* encyclopedia, there is a photo of lines of black boys in Africa going through ritual circumcision. They endure this with no anesthetic.

He could not bear it with their courage. He would cry and wail. He would have to be dragged kicking and screaming to the place, just as he is to school, before anyone was allowed to do that to him.

Of course, what he wants to see, but the photo does not show, is the fact of the knife cutting through flesh. Instead, he must make do with the grim resolution on these boys' faces. The book makes no mention of what happens to the boys who fail this rite, this test of their manhood. It does not say, he suspects, because the truth is too awful: that those who fail are castrated altogether. To fail this test would mean failure to become a man.

His father is circumcised. He has seen his father's penis, every morning when he walks back to the bedroom from the bathroom, dark and weathered like an acorn. He wishes his father did not walk naked around the house. It is not nice. If he looked like his father, he would always keep his clothes on.

The question he dares not ask, dares not even think, is this: what if he does not grow into a man? What if, amidst all the ways he is odd, puberty is another? His sister has grown, even though she is a year younger than he is. She and her friend, Jade, now stand a few inches taller than him. Whereas before, Jade would come over and the three of them would play together, now the two girls disappear off without him, speaking in hushed tones designed to exclude him.

Family friends will chorus about how tall his sister is, before thoughtful ones tell him that girls grow earlier than boys. While kindly meant, he finds this concession humiliating. He does not want their sympathy, he does not want them to draw attention to it, does not want what is obvious to him to be obvious to everyone else too: that he is not doing what he should be doing, and that in some way, his younger sister has supplanted him.

At the end of the following school year, he will move to senior school. He does not want to go to senior school, although he cannot say why. As much as he doesn't like school, he does not want, nor see, why things must change. He would much rather things remain exactly as they are. Peter Pan never grew up but that was because he was lost.

He knows growing up has something to do with sex.

However, he does not find sex a sufficient justification. Sex is to do with getting married and having a family. But he already has a family. Why can't everyone stay in their existing families?

Already in his class there is one boy, Morrow, clearly marked by puberty. He is now a whole head taller than everyone else, including the boys who used to be tall. He has fair, downy hair on his face and the boy notices, when they change for games, the penis that has swelled between Morrow's legs. How, he wonders, should this happen? It is as though this boy has inflated his child's penis like a balloon. What must he do for the same to happen to him?

While he beats Morrow in every class they share, Morrow seems blissfully ignorant of the competition that exists between them. Or, if he is aware, then it is not a competition he cares for.

He fears Morrow's mind is elsewhere. That, somehow, something about their rivalry and his own investment in it is childish. Morrow's behavior suggests that, if only he were to grow up, he would see how trivial everything else is: what use is a ninety in maths if his voice has not broken? Of all the competitions, sex is the only one that matters and, in that, Morrow is winning.

He feels his lateness in starting puberty must have something to do with him. His own insufficiency. Given he is eating extra greens, drinking a pint of milk each evening, but has yet to start his growth spurt, then, is it possible, there is some willful part of him that will not grow? He should be able to will his body any way he wants. What is the point of a body if it has a mind of its own? In this, too, he will not behave as he should.

When one of the boys in his year, a fat child who amuses himself by belching in people's faces, brings a porn mag into school, he cannot understand the clamor to see it. He is disgusted: by the nakedness, by the bodily fluids, the way the images are staged. There is nothing artful, beautiful nor romantic about them. There is nothing in this ritual to appeal to him. It is animal.

It is the same order of behavior he shrinks from when this boy belches in his face: a guttural, gassy noise accompanied by a sweet acidic tang. He does not want to be forced to smell this boy's digestive process; he does not want to consider any bodily processes. Ideally, he'd like to forget he has a body altogether.

What is worse is the way his classmates, his friends, respond to the magazine. And yet, he doesn't want his peers to think him frigid. He knows that while it is bad for a girl, a woman, to be called frigid, it is utterly unthinkable for a man. A man must have a passionate nature. It is his duty. To fail as a lover is to fail at the very core of what it means to be a man. So reluctantly he joins the huddle around the desk. He joins in the talk, all the while believing that no one—no one but the most depraved—could ever do such absurd things.

He is shocked when Philip confides how he'd like to

"fuck," shocked that Philip should also want this huffing and puffing. He cannot understand why anyone would own up to this. At most he imagines it like an itch. Everyone is shamed by their desire, he reasons, because it is coarse and brutish. If only we could cut it off, excise it altogether; how much better we could be then.

And yet, what if this difference really speaks of something wrong with him? Perhaps, far from being noble, he is incapable of the grand emotions penned by Shakespeare. Instead he is just a prig, a child, a dried-up husk, like a woodlouse with a mouthful of sawdust.

He wants to be a great lover, the kind immortalized in full-length portraits or poems. He knows his father is not a capable lover—his mother has said so—and this does not surprise him. He could have guessed. His father is not worthy of the grand, eloquent love of poetry. When his mother tells him the story of their honeymoon, on the same island they go to every year, she says she was left unfulfilled.

"It was my first time," she told him. "Frankly, I expected more."

What she does not address, but he knows from another of his parents' stories, is that this is also the night they claim he was conceived. He is concerned the stain of unsatisfactory lovemaking should have attached to him somehow, depriving him of something vital. If the way you are got sets the tone of your life, defines your nature, perhaps a passionless conception explains him? His uncertainty, his doubt, the way he must interrogate everything, are all these symptoms of the same doubt, the lack, with which he was got? Is this the way he is marked?

౿ᏒᏱ

When watching the motor racing, he always supports Jacques Villeneuve. While in almost every respect they are different, Jacques Villeneuve is short and he is short too. In this simple way he feels he and Jacques Villeneuve are brothers.

When Jacques Villeneuve turns up at the French Grand Prix with bleached hair this causes minor outrage among the assembled press. This is not the behavior of a serious sportsman, as the TV commentator informs him. It is not the behavior of someone taking their corporate role within a team seriously. Not the behavior of one committed to becoming world champion.

He tells his mother he would like bleached hair. She tells him this is not possible. He would not be allowed it for school. Fine, he says, then he will get his hair bleached at the start of the school holidays.

No more is said about it. He takes this as his mother's acceptance. She speaks with his father, but his father does not join in. He does at least credit his father with treating him like an adult, even while he suspects his father simply cannot be bothered with the argument. This standoff is between him and his mother. He suspects that neither of his parents believes he will do it. In truth, he does not believe he will do it either.

When the school holidays begin, he announces his intention to go into town. He will go to the hairdressers, he says. His mother tells him no one is going into town that afternoon so he won't be able to get a lift. Were he another boy he might challenge this, challenge it by saying he will cycle the six miles. That is what Philip would do. That is the kind of boy he ought to be. But in this she has defeated him. She knows he does not have the stomach for it, knows exactly what kind of boy he is, despite his best attempts to deceive her.

At the start of the following week his mother plays her trump card. She has been speaking to their gardener, Malcolm. His father disapproves of Malcolm—Malcolm claims unemployment benefit while working several jobs. Malcolm has told her that bleached hair is a signal.

"On the housing estate," his mother tells him, "bleached hair is a homosexual code. It is a code between homosexuals and it indicates between them that you are the receiving party."

That is the phrase his mother uses: receiving party.

He wonders how Malcolm knows this. How do adults learn of these secret codes?

"Is that," his mother asks, "the message that you wish to give out?" She adds, "Do you want people going about town, people on the estate going around thinking you want them to do that to you?"

He does not. However, he does not know why such an idea should attach to him, or indeed to the men with bleached hair on the housing estate, but not to Jacques Villeneuve. If it should apply to some, then it should apply to all. There is an inconsistency, an arbitrariness, he does not understand. All the same, he does not go, and is grateful to his mother for saving him any embarrassment.

Chapter 14

Over the summer, they return to Cornwall. However, this year their week is wet, they are confined to the cottage. The sun cannot break through heavy clouds, the garden is dark and imposing, thick with shrubs and trees. Their father builds a log fire, and they gather around the living-room table and play cards: rounds of snap and clock patience, in which his sister always wins. They undertake a thousand-piece jigsaw with their mother—two contrasting scenes of soldiers heading to France from Waterloo Station. He likes the intimacy of the jigsaw, a closeness in the silence, one he can almost breathe himself into.

He takes himself off and reads on the settle among the coats and boots. Hidden away, his feet up, huddled to the radiator, he devotes himself to a copy of *Nineteen Eighty-Four* he found on the cottage bookshelves.

During the day they will brave the wind and rain to

get tea on the quay, scones and cream and Victoria sponge cake dusted with icing sugar, and argue over whether it's too cold for ice cream. Rain and fog mean they can see nothing beyond the swell of the sea, not even the short distance across the channel to the island opposite. On the beach, salt water whips and burns their skin, while their mother stops and points out a fishing boat, struggling into port.

Back home, he and his sister race along the country roads, standing on their pedals to see out over the hedges and across the fields, tall with grass. A kestrel hangs over the verge before falling from the sky. They make the climb up to the post office in the neighboring village and race back down the sunken lane, through a tunnel of trees, their roots a straggly wall either side. He does not want to return to school. He would rather stop, disappear deep within the hedgerows.

He and Philip begin confirmation classes, along with one other boy from their year, and two from different schools. These other boys are at senior school already and do not talk to them as they wait outside the rectory, only to each other. When the vicar opens the door with a bow, the older boys enter first.

He does not know why Philip is here. Philip's family does not go to church, he is allowed to stay at home and watch cartoons instead. He suspects it is because, in one of their extra lessons, Mr. Miller described confirmation as a rite of passage. Yet, as far as he is aware, he is the only one at confirmation class to go to church—this, he feels, should be the true test for confirmation, not classes of an hour over a mere eight weeks. The rectory is large and cold. Each week, they huddle in a group in a side room. The vicar, a young man with a face like a spoon, gets up intermittently to check that the electric heater is on before rubbing his hands together and sitting back down.

In the first week, they are each presented with a slim, orange volume of Mark's Gospel. They are to study this over the classes.

He knows that when their time is up, when they are confirmed, they will finally be able to receive Holy Communion. That is why he is here. That is the purpose of confirmation. However, midway through these evening classes he has a question. He has read ahead in Mark's Gospel, he tells the vicar, but he can find no mention of confirmation.

"Is it in the other gospels?" he asks. "The confirmation of the disciples?"

"No," the vicar tells him—confirmation is a later invention of the Church. A sacrament designed to confirm those baptized in their faith.

Why then, he asks, must *they* be confirmed before receiving Holy Communion?

He senses the other boys resent his questions. There is an agenda for the class and he is taking them off it. One of the older boys stares at him, before saying these things are as they are, and not to question it. But he is not cowed. Isn't questioning the point of these classes? he asks the vicar. To which the vicar responds that it is, but so too is faith. He does not understand this reply. He feels it a cheat. A cheap way of being told there are certain questions that can be asked and others that cannot.

At the end of the class he asks to stay behind. The vicar bows to the other four at the door before turning back to him. He senses everyone is a little annoyed— that somehow he isn't quite playing the game.

"It says in the Bible," he begins, sitting awkwardly on the edge of a sofa, "and in the Eucharist, that communion is God's gift to us. Is that right?"

"It is," replies the vicar.

Then why, he asks, can't he have it now? Why, if it is a gift from God, has the Church put a barrier in the way of his receiving it? If it is a gift from God, then no one should step in between him and receiving what is rightfully his.

The vicar asks if he thinks it is important that everyone knows what they are signing up for. That, if people are to receive a gift, it is done in good grace and they are aware of what is being given. Would it not be wrong merely to go through the motions, ignorant?

He agrees it would be. This, he thinks but does not say, is what Philip and the others are doing. Why should he, who goes to church every week, find himself challenged by questions, while they, who have no interest at all, are spared?

But he does not say this, instead he restates that, while no one should go through the motions, confirmation could happen anyway without the carrot of communion at the end of it. Who are these people coming between him and God like this? Who do they think they are?

They are the elders of the Church. Founders of the faith, he is told.

He would like to ask more but the vicar rises at this point, says he must get on.

"Your mother is surely waiting," he says. He adds that he hopes these concerns can be set aside.

That evening, his mother mentions in passing that, following the service, there are to be photos kept at the back of the abbey of all the confirmation candidates. He doesn't like this. He doesn't like having his photo taken, the image given to him bears no resemblance to how he sees himself: an impostor has been put there in his stead. His mother tells him he is being ridiculous. Everyone will have their photo taken, it is a trivial thing, it really does not matter. But he is insistent: he does not want a photo taken of himself and then placed at the back of the abbey for everyone to gawp at. He does not want to be singled out. Had he known this when he agreed to get confirmed then he would have felt differently.

The following week, the vicar asks them to name

their favorite disciple. Philip names Peter and the vicar nods in assent.

"Peter is a very good choice." Peter is his favorite also, the vicar says. "Peter aspires to be better than he is but, ultimately, like all of us, he is flawed."

"My favorite is Judas," the boy announces.

"Of course he is," the vicar replies. "And why is Judas your favorite?"

"Because Judas was right."

"In what way was he right? Why is the man who betrayed the Son of God your favorite? Why not choose one of the good, loyal ones, like Peter or Andrew or James or John, as your classmates have done?"

"Jesus said there will be poor always and Judas said that wasn't fair. And he was right. If you are God then there shouldn't be poor always."

"All right. But is that enough reason to betray the Son of God?"

"I feel sorry for him too," the boy adds. "Jesus kept getting angry and shouting at people and Judas wanted him to be better. Someone had to betray Jesus. Judas was just doing what someone had to do."

"I'm not sure that stands up to our having free will, Daniel. Judas made a choice, like we all can. He also chose to kill himself. Readers of the Bible would understand that as a sin, as the coward's way out—"

"Jesus is the coward," he interrupts, not sure why he has got so involved. Involved and angry. "Jesus is the coward because he loses his temper but tells people off for doing the same. Jesus says there'll be poor always just so he can get his feet washed. And someone had to betray him and if he was God he would have known that, he would have made it happen. So Judas had no choice. And still he was punished for it, which isn't fair. And if God is all loving then he would forgive Judas anyway, especially as he killed himself. So I like Judas best because he was honest. He was honest and sad and he believed in a better world than Jesus did. A better world than God."

Over the following days he reaches a decision. He cannot be confirmed. He does not want to sign up to something he believes to be wrong, and to have his communion withheld seems to him to be wrong. This has also set other doubts in motion. If these elders institute arbitrary measures like this, then what else have they inserted without his knowledge? What other prescriptions is he being forced to accept?

He tells his parents and the vicar of his decision. The vicar expresses his sadness and asks him to reconsider. But he will not.

"When I'm allowed to receive communion, then I will get confirmed," he says.

The vicar says he has it the wrong way round. Besides, does he not see that by denying confirmation he is denying himself communion? He cannot help that, he replies. It is the Church denying him communion. He cannot sign up to something he believes to be unjust.

His father says little; his mother tells him he is cutting off his nose to spite his face. Mr. Miller calls him Martin Luther, before telling him to not be so self-aggrandizing. He is surprised at this, surprised at his mother. He'd expected, given what she says about the village church being close-minded for not welcoming children, that she would support him.

"I've spoken with the vicar," she tells him later, "and he says you don't have to have your photo taken if you don't want to." She smiles as though she has made him some gift.

"But I'm not getting confirmed."

"Well I know you *weren't*, but, as they've said you don't need to have your photograph taken, now you can."

He is incensed. How can she have such a low opinion of him? He flies into a rage. Is this what she thinks of him? That he would take a stand, refuse confirmation, out of sheer vanity at not liking his photo being taken? He doesn't give her a chance to reply because he feels sure if she did, she would only confirm that yes, she really does think him that petty and childish.

Above all, why does no one seem to think his taking a stand a good thing? He could have accepted everything without question. He could have made life easy for himself. Instead, he seems to be the only one asking questions. Is this not exactly what Jesus would have done? he asks his parents. His mother does not welcome the comparison.

"But why are they all being rewarded?" he says of the others. "They haven't asked any questions. Philip doesn't even go to church. Why do they get to be confirmed, and be given presents and have communion when they've not asked any questions? Why don't they care?"

He still attends the confirmation service, which takes place after half term. He would rather not but his mother says he must, that he should support Philip. She also needles him that he must feel sorry, left out, when he could be taking part. He does not feel left out, for he has taken a stand. However, he is anxious that everyone knows and judges him accordingly: he is the difficult boy who has an argument with the Church, who feels it his place to question the elders.

The service takes place and afterward he gives each of the others a card. One of the older boys, the one who stared him down, shrugs with disinterest.

"Why are you here?" the older boy demands. "Why aren't you getting confirmed?"

He didn't expect to have the matter raised so directly. He does not wish to justify himself to others publicly. He is caught off guard. He stammers that he believes the Church's position on confirmation a little confused.

"I think you're the one who's confused," the other snaps back, one corner of his mouth twisted into a half smile.

He feels this injustice deeply. It is not I who am confused, he wants to say. I am the only one thinking clearly.

Why have you signed up to a system that stops you receiving what is yours by right? But he does not think to say any of this in time.

He gives Philip his card but Philip is immediately whisked away by his mother. Is that how things are to be now, he wonders. Will he and Philip no longer speak because he is a religious pariah?

On Sunday he announces that he will no longer be going to church. His mother is aghast. She tells him he must go. Philip doesn't go to church, he says. That's Philip's business, she tells him, and Philip's parents'." She does not know why Philip's parents do not make him attend church.

Maybe Philip doesn't believe in God, he suggests. And maybe Philip is right. Maybe there is no God, or, if there is, he is not worth bothering with. Philip must believe in God, she says, because Philip has just been confirmed. Fine, he replies, but I don't want to go to an Anglican church anymore. I don't agree with their view on confirmation. Fine, she replies, but in that case, he must decide what denomination he will choose.

He thinks this over. It is quite clear that he cannot be Catholic. The Catholics are even worse than the Anglicans, that much he has gathered. He tells his parents he does not see why anyone should have to go to church. Why can't he say his prayers out in a field? Why must they go to a gray, drafty building every week when they could be outside? His mother buttons her coat and tells him they do not have time for this—they are late. He refuses to move. Fine, he can miss church this week but next week he must attend church. His sister demands that she be allowed off as well.

"He is not being allowed off," his mother says. "He's thinking very hard about where to go to church."

His sister insists that she is doing the same.

He resents his sister. She is not thinking about denominations, she is merely copying him so she can stay at home and watch cartoons. Worse still, by copying him she is undermining his argument. As long as neither of them go to church his mother has a better argument for forcing them both.

The following week he tells his father he would like to attend a Methodist service. He understands that Methodist churches are simpler, without all the decoration, without a choir. The early Methodists had their services out in fields, led by a man on horseback. The Methodists challenged the elders of the church, they did not just accept what they were told. He can get behind the Methodists. The Methodists do not allow things to get in the way of you and God. This is what he wants. He will be a Methodist.

His father drives him into town on Sunday. He is disappointed to find that the Methodists still have their services inside. As they enter, a woman, the wife of one of his teachers, greets them with a smile. But he must confess he is disappointed. No one else welcomes them.

Worse still, the building is red brick, with pine pews. It looks like a village hall, with none of the grandeur of the abbey. As much as he wants to be away from the abbey, this is not what he expected.

He and his father are ushered to seats near the back. There are hymns but they come in a different book than he is used to; this one is soft-bound, with a rainbow on the cover. He does not want a children's book in church.

After the service he tells his father he does not think he is a Methodist. What other denominations are there? His father tells him about the Baptists. The Baptists allow everyone to receive communion. Fine, he says, then he is a Baptist. However, something in his father's voice does not make him warm to the Baptists. He is also anxious that at some point he will be forced underwater. He does not see how being forced underwater to become a Baptist is any better than being forced to be confirmed in order to receive Holy Communion.

Then there are the Quakers. The Quakers do not meet in church but in people's houses. They do not have the rituals he dislikes, there are no rules regarding communion. The Quakers meet and discuss, they are much more accommodating of dissenting views. On this basis, he decides that the Quakers are very sensible people. He could be a Quaker.

"Do they go outside?" he asks.

His father is not sure. "Possibly, but usually they meet in one another's homes or a special meeting house."

However, given his experience of the Methodists, he suspects he would dislike a meeting house even more than a church. If he must be kept inside, he would far rather it felt like a church than a village hall or someone's living room. How are you meant to consider the divine, sat on a sofa with a TV standby light winking at you?

If he cannot reconcile himself to a Christian god, then is it because he is not even a Christian? Might he be a Jew? Or a Muslim?

He sees that part of his problem is that he does not know how to choose. Worst of all, every choice means giving something up. He does not want to give anything up. He does not see why he should.

He wonders why this should all be so difficult. How is he to choose without some sort of divine sign? And how is it that other people know these things without a sign? Does Philip know, or does he simply not care? Has no one else asked these questions either? He does not see why he should be in such anguish for taking these matters seriously. He does not want to be troubled by asking questions of the universe and existence. Above all else, he wants to be left alone.

Chapter 15

At Christmas, he and his sister make paper chains in front of the fire, a tub of Quality Street by their side. He wants snow but instead there is a heavy frost, which casts a crisp, brittle tinge over the world on the other side of the icy windows.

A series of visitors comes to the front door, some with gifts, all addressed to his father. He and his sister dutifully place these under the tree along with any packages brought by the postman. The boy will wrap the latter in bright Christmas paper to hide the brown parcel paper beneath.

His mother gives him a video of *Tom Brown's Schooldays*. He does not tell her that this black-and-white film, a "U" certificate, gives him nightmares about starting senior school. He is menaced by the opening credits, with their bright and resolute violins, and the boisterous singing of Latin. He doesn't know what he feels threatened by, nor why he feels out of place, only that he does not feel what he ought to feel.

Perhaps it is that Tom Brown follows his feelings and the unwritten code of boys. He knows himself to be subject to this code, yet he is not privy to it at the same time. The jeers and taunts, the punches he has received, show he has broken the code while neither knowing nor understanding it. This is the same code Mr. Miller invokes when calling him a prig, a swot, a goody-goody, and a show-off. Yet Philip and the others seem to understand well enough, understand without needing to be told.

He will not be Tom, he will end up as George Arthur. Tom is unnaturally good, with a drooping upper lip, like a hanging apostrophe. The destiny of Tom is to thrive, the destiny of poor Arthur to perish. And maybe this is it: that Philip, like Tom, gets on, while, somehow, he does not. He will not leave things alone, he must worry everything. Rather than accepting things, he only ever wants to question them.

When out shopping with his father and sister during the holidays, they leave the butchers and are accosted by a woman in the street. He hears her before he sees her, her voice incoherent but loud. She sobs between shouts.

"Daddy, what's wrong with that lady?" he asks.

"She's homeless," his father says.

Why does she have no home? he wonders. Is there no one who can help her? No one who can take her in? Can she stay with them? His father says no.

She asks for money, a dirty hand held out from between the gaps of the sleeping bag wrapped round her, but they push on, the three of them; they walk away. Shouts come from behind, shouts of abuse. It is like the boys in the street.

"You can't help everybody," his father tells him, and yet he is left wondering why not.

He hates his father for not helping, for not offering to take her in, for not alleviating her suffering. However, he resents the woman too. He is bothered by the memory of her that evening at home, by her crying, for the words she poured out at their departing backs. Maybe he is also a little relieved that, unlike his mother, there are people his father will not help. He does not get drawn in by people. He has boundaries.

At the start of the new term, after morning service, he takes the chance to speak with the vicar about what his father has said. The floods are up, and this means he will have to walk the long way back to school alone, but there is no one else he can think to ask. He feels sure the vicar will side with him over his father.

Yet the vicar tells him, "You cannot take the weight of the world on your shoulders. It is not up to you to save the world."

Whose job is it to save the world then? he wonders. If everyone felt like the vicar, then surely nothing would ever change?

The vicar gestures for him to take one of the empty seats at the back of the nave. They sit alone, as the sun pours through the stained-glass windows so the colors spiral across the yellow flagstone floor. The vicar tells him the story of a poet; a poet who wrote that, rather than saving the world, we should each clear a small space in the forest of our lives, then hold open our hands and wait for the song of ourselves to land there.

He does not understand what this means. "If you sit in the forest and hold out your hands, you're not doing anything," he says. "That doesn't help anybody. They couldn't do that in the war."

"That is true," the vicar replies, bowing his head. "There are always things we have to do, but there comes a time when we must stop, when there is nothing we can do."

He does not agree. He is quite happy that saving the world should not solely be down to him, but neither does it seem true that it is not down to him at all. The only way that saving the world should not solely be down to him is if it were down to everybody. He does not see how this can be advanced by people sitting in the forest of themselves with their cupped hands outstretched.

Looking down at his own shoes, small and scuffed next to the vicar's adult, polished leather, he ponders another question. "How is life fair if we can't be as we want? If we try hard enough?" he adds. "I mean, why shouldn't my mum be a great actress if she wants to be? Or that lady not be homeless but happy and with a family? Why can't we be as we choose?"

"Because life doesn't work like that, Daniel. Some things are the way they are."

"But if none of us can be as we want, then what is the point in anything?" He cannot believe his life should be prescribed for him, written out already.

"I don't think it works like that. God doesn't work like that."

At home, his mother asks about his day and then if anything is wrong, if someone has been mean to him. She always asks this, and he hates that his vulnerability should be so starkly legible.

He tells her of his conversation with the vicar. Why, he asks, can't he be more like Philip? Why won't his father play football or cricket with him, like the other boys' fathers? Why can't he be the tallest in class?

"You can't do that, Daniel. You can't decide to be tall or decide to be good at cricket."

"Why not?"

"Because that's not how life works. There are some things you just have to accept."

"Well, I won't. I won't accept anything. If I will it, then it will be so. I will make it so. It's not fair that some people get everything and other people nothing," he adds.

"It's not about what you get," his mother replies. "It's about what you do with it. You can make the best of it, you can be generous with what you have, or you can resent it and make nothing of what you've got. There's no point in comparing yourself with Philip, because you and Philip are different people, with different needs and different talents and different histories. You can't go around comparing yourself to other people all the time—it will only make you miserable."

"But it's not fair!"

"Life isn't fair, Daniel!"

This is one of her cop-out answers. It is not good enough to say life isn't fair. Even if it isn't, then it should be. Is it not her job to make it fair? Or, if there is a God, that he should make things fair? Most importantly of all, if there is no God, isn't it up to everyone to try and make things fairer?

"He should make it so that you are happy and not depressed," he adds, "and so that everyone has a talent and so that people can grow tall and everyone can be free to be as they want to be."

"But you can't do all of this on your own, Daniel."

What he'd like to say is that of course this is true, and if only other people pulled their weight, then he wouldn't be doing it on his own. Isn't the very fact, however, that he is trying, that he is prepared to risk doing it on his own, with no prospect of fairness, a good thing? Doesn't that suggest something special about him?

"No," his mother says. "Then you are only doing it to seem special."

Chapter 16

He is descended from kings. His uncle traced the family history back to the civil war—then a gap—and then lineage right back to 1066. Were it not for this gap, they could be somebody. Previously, he copied out his uncle's research into a hardback notebook with a cover of faux leather he was given one birthday. "Volume 1" is written in a calligraphic script on the inside cover and, while embarrassed at his childish pretension, he approves of the sentiment. His family's greatness should not merely be confined to one volume.

It cannot be up to his father. They were somebody before his father lost everything—they had a position in town, people knew who they were. His father concedes as much on the many occasions he apologizes for their loss of the big house. If they were somebody now, he could believe his family mattered.

But slowly he gets to wondering, could his bond with

Philip suggest that Philip is a part of his family, that Philip is part of his inheritance too? Who would he be if family trees were drawn not in lines of blood, but through what is shared? Then whose son would he be?

However, when he asks his mother, she is adamant.

"No, Daniel," she says. "There are such things as facts. Philip is a friend. Mr. Miller can be a friend or a mentor. But they are not family. They do not look after you, they do not care for you. They do not have the same kind of duty to you as we do, as your family does."

"I think we should have a duty to everybody," he pronounces. "A duty to everybody, but our family should be those we have most in common with."

"That is a different thing," his mother says. "Family is important. Family is made of blood."

He is not interested in blood, although he does not say this. He is squeamish. If he cuts himself, he faints. What he is interested in are words. Words and marks on paper, made by a pen or brush. These are what matter.

Family is quaint, an animal thing. It is the same as the business with the sheep outside, the ducks in the paddock and the dog and her litter in the kennel. It is about bloodlines and reproduction, and this strikes him as distasteful, primitive, from another time, like the getting and begetting of stock.

He wonders about voice parts, whether he will follow his father. His father sang in the choir, but this carries no weight with him. He will not bring it up because his father sang alto and he feels this to be an unmanly thing for his father to have done. His father boasts of the high notes he was able to sing at university, notes usually only attainable by women or young boys, notes high enough that they excited the music master of his college. His father regales visitors to the house with these stories. He, on the other hand, will blush on his father's behalf that he should so readily reveal his lack of manly vigor. It is no wonder his mother has the better of him.

Walking out on their break, along the narrow road that passes over the stream and onto the large common land, known as the vineyards, the boys ask Mr. Miller what voice parts each of them will have. No one ever questions the lack of vines on the vineyards, nor why this expanse of ground, always a dark green from the many months under the spring floodwaters, should have that name.

As Mr. Miller also sings in the choir, presumably he has some insight as to how voice parts are determined. Not only that, but as they fire questions at the teacher it is as though this is something to be known, to be ordained. While the whole school files out in the midmorning sun, everyone else is in an orderly line but for the four boys, gathered around the teacher, a raucous bunch, joshing and practicing voices that are as low as they can go.

Philip says he will be a bass and Mr. Miller points at him and says, "Bass!"

The boy knows that Mr. Miller is a tenor. He would

like to be like Mr. Miller. His father has told him that tenors are rare.

"I want to be a tenor," he says.

"Not a bass like Philip?"

"No, a tenor."

"I'm a tenor," Mr. Miller says.

"I know," replies the boy. "I want to be a tenor like you. Tenors are the most prized."

"A tenor is a lovely voice," Mr. Miller says. "Yes," he adds emphatically, "you can be a tenor!"

He is aware, from his father, that becoming one of these parts has something to do with becoming a man. Yet he disdains his father's crass talk, the way he will ask the choirmaster which boys have had to leave the choir "because their balls have dropped." He does not believe that the choirmaster and his father should speak in such terms, with language that conjures images of pubescent genitals into his head and, presumably, into theirs also.

What disturbs him most is the thought that they might speak of him in these terms. Are his body, his voice, his genitals, so readily assessed and accessible to the minds of others? He does not want anyone thinking, or knowing, such things about him.

To him, a voice part is a choice. During puberty, he reckons something forms in growing testicles that coats and thickens the vocal cords. A bass will be one who has had the most of this substance and therefore whose vocal cords have thickened the most, like the fat string of a double bass.

If he wants to be a tenor, then he will be a tenor. If he were to become an alto like his father, it would mean nothing other than a lack of conviction on his part. Equally, as his voice represents him, speaks of him irrespective of the words he utters, then he must have mastery over it. His body should not be capable of defying him.

Neither does he see how his name—the words attached to him—represent him. His name is not even his own but his father's—his father's but less. It is a shadow of a name. When he spells it out, thinks on it, reflects on the run of sounds that makes up his name, it is trivial. These utterances do not describe him—they reduce him. This is not who he is.

He has argued with Mr. Miller over what it means to represent something, when he says how much he likes Constable's *The Hay Wain* during one of their general art classes. He is attracted to the wateriness of the scene, with the rickety cart making its way through the overflowing stream. Mr. Miller does not share his enthusiasm. In fact, he has clearly made a significant error of taste. Mr. Miller takes it up in front of the other children.

"I love *The Hay Wain*!" he mimics in a high, reedy voice, to sniggers from the class.

The other day his picture was wrong because it failed to resemble life, so he cannot see why he should be in error now for liking something that best resembles the original.

Instead, the master lays out paint-flecked postcards by Raoul Dufy, bright colors and gondolas scribbled in pen and ink that bob like melon slices on Venice canals. He does not know why this should be better, why one minute he should be urged to observe closely, if the next he is to forget all that, and be asked to draw like a child.

"But it doesn't look like that," the boy exclaims.

"That doesn't matter," Mr. Miller snaps. "There are more important things than representation."

"Like what?"

"Like truth."

He does not understand this. If a thing does not look like what it is, then that is a lie.

No, the teacher tells him. "Reality and truth are not the same thing."

"But the water isn't red!" he exclaims. "And a boat doesn't look like that. *The Hay Wain*—" But before he can finish, Mr. Miller is off again.

"*The Hay Wain! The Hay Wain!*" he cries. "You want everything to look like a chocolate box. You just copy your parents' bourgeois, provincial tastes!"

He has learned to be wary of Mr. Miller on days like this, when he comes in wearing a silk handkerchief tucked about his collar. Then the master will speak with a flourish, as though pulling the handkerchief from round his neck, but a flourish that is cruel.

However, later that week he fails to take heed, as Mr. Miller pulls at the silk and plumps it around his collar in one of their extra art classes. Following the boy's account of his mother's retelling of *Romeo and Juliet*, the master tells him the story of *Hamlet*. This excites him even more—the Danish prince who struggles and contemplates alone seems to him a higher order of person than loved-up teenagers. That you would kill to honor your father's memory strikes him as more probable than an obscure feud between families. Mr. Miller also tells him about Lear—that *King Lear* is the greatest of the plays—but he cannot feel this, he has no interest in an old man who wanders around making stupid decisions. No, it is the Dane who speaks to him.

Looking to impress by demonstrating his wide cultural knowledge, he mentions hearing that *Romeo and Juliet* has been retold in song. What could be finer, the boy suggests, than to tell the story with songs, with dancing? How much more it all is. But the teacher does not share his excitement.

"Musicals are naff, ephemeral," he tells the boy flatly. "They do not meet the standard of great art."

"But aren't they like plays only with music?"

"They're not opera, if that's what you mean," Mr. Miller says, raising his voice. "They are cheap and sentimental."

"What does sentimental mean?"

"It means generating feelings in a way that is easy

and self-indulgent. Rather than genuinely feeling an emotion, you contrive it just to say you have had it."

"Is that bad?"

"It is when it's excessive or cheap. There is feeling that is profound and deep, that is truly affecting. And then there is feeling that is shallow. That does none of the work. Think of greetings cards on Valentine's Day with mawkish, printed messages and badly drawn flowers— all done for the sender. There is no real feeling there. It is sentimental—cliché. Musicals are like that. They are easily got. There is something feminine about them altogether. Unnatural."

The master goes quiet, seemingly lost in his own painting, the one he is doing alongside the boy. And then he gathers up the brushes and drops them all in the sink.

The boy feels the clatter of the brushes, one after the other, a rapping at his head. And at once, the mood of the room changes, like the snap of an elastic band.

"You should watch that you—yourself—aren't cheap," Mr. Miller says, his back still to him. "You are too given to histrionics," he tells him, finally turning around, using a paper towel to dry his hands and forearms. "Like your mother."

"What does that mean?" he asks.

"It means exaggerated, theatrical, stagy."

This isn't what he meant. He wants to know what is wrong with him. Him and his mother. Although he suspects, and feels his ears burn red.

"If I want to be on stage," he protests, "or be an artist, it must be good to be stagy."

"No, it isn't," Mr. Miller tells him. "It's too much."

"But *you* are theatrical," the boy reasons. It is one of the things he likes about the teacher. But this only seems to make him flare up all the more.

"It is not good!" snaps Mr. Miller. "It might be good when on stage. It is not good to be stagy in everyday life. And, arguably, it is not good to be stagy on stage either."

"Why not?"

"Because acting—art—should convince and be believable. You are not believable if you're being stagy. You're just showing off."

He does not know how he is meant to see things the way Mr. Miller does.

"If you like *The Hay Wain*," the master adds, "then maybe you shouldn't be in extra art. Maybe you should be with all the others."

Sure enough, when he next has art with the rest of his year, he is abandoned to the others and their poster paints. Only Philip works directly under Mr. Miller, as the teacher's hand guides Philip's in caresses across the paper.

He has never felt a loss like it. Not even when they lost the cat. The poster paints are crass and childish. He can do nothing with them but blocks and shapes that merge together. His classmates glory in his demotion. "*The Hay Wain! The Hay Wain!*" they parrot. He does not understand how to have an adult taste, the taste of his parents, can render him childish. He tries. The harder he tries to remonstrate with the teacher, the worse he makes it.

"So what? What do you like?" Mr. Miller demands, an audience gathering around him.

"I like that it looks like what it is!"

"How do you know?" the teacher demands. "Look! Look—it's all muddy browns. Have you ever seen a scene like that? What about the experience of a scene? The hot heat of a summer day?"

"But that one"—he points to one of the postcards—"is silly. The buildings are pink and they all lean over and—"

"I like *The Hay Wain!*" the chorus begins again.

When the class is dismissed, he holds up his work for the usual "The boy's a genius," but none comes, only a cursory glance.

Over the next four weeks he must go out to games with everyone else. He stands alone on the touchline, kicking his muddy boots together. The ball never comes to him, and, for this, he is glad.

Philip is not at games. Philip remains in the art room. Why should Philip, who likes games, who does not even care about art, be the one chosen for this extra time all to himself?

He, on the other hand, must be an artist or nothing else explains him. If he is stagy and showing off, then he must also be special. He needs Mr. Miller. If anyone can make him normal, like Philip, while nurturing his greatness, then it is he.

At home he asks his mother, "Was Jesus showing off?"

"No, he wasn't. He could do the things he said he could do."

"Well, maybe I can do the things I say I can do. How am I to know without trying?"

"There are some things it is not possible to do."

"But I can still try."

"You can't, Daniel. There are some things that are simply facts. You can't fly, for example."

"I don't mean flying. I mean being what I want. What I *am*."

"You can't make yourself just how you want to be. Or what someone else wants you to be, either," she adds. "You have no control over what others think of you."

"No, but I can control how and who I am. I will be like everyone else. The only way I will be different is by being special. And I will be special by being exactly as I want."

"You can't be like everyone else *and* special. If someone is special, then they are not like everyone else."

Philip confides to him that he would rather they still had art together. He is bored on his own, it is no fun without him. If he is to be on his own, he would rather be out at games with everyone else.

When the month is up, Mr. Miller relents and he is returned to the art room.

"Your friend is a good friend to you," he says.

The boy smiles weakly. If he is to be readmitted, he would like it to be for his own sake.

Finally, he and Mr. Miller are reconciled. They are alone today, for Philip is out at games, and he feels hopeful somehow at this chance to have the teacher to himself. They scour a new set of postcards: dark, Gothic ruins by John Piper. Something ominous in rough pen—hallowed spaces that threaten more than they promise, ruined walls bleached bright by the sun, against a dark, forbidding sky. The postcards set out are not his inspiration but simply the master copy he is to redraft. To imitate is, frankly, all they are ever asked to do.

While he works, Mr. Miller takes all the art materials from the wardrobe and lays them out across the other table: boxes of pastels, bunches of charcoal, metal tubes of acrylic and watercolor, artist's pencils, brand new, their points sharp and all equal length. As he tidies the cupboard, the boy works on in silence; he hadn't realized silence could be a balm, believing it to be a cold or an angry thing, or at least having found it so with anyone but Philip. But the pair of them are oblivious to the departure and later the return of everyone from the games fields, and later still when the light outside cools and there is the gentle patter of voices as parents arrive for collection.

"It's getting late. You should have gone already," the

man finally says. "You've done good work today, Peter Pan!" and the boy gives him a high five, before gathering up his things.

"I've been impressed with you this afternoon," Mr. Miller continues. "If you can keep working like this—" But he doesn't finish the sentence.

He smiles.

"You'd get on so much better with everyone if you always worked like this," he adds.

"What do you mean?"

"If you just rubbed along with people a little more," the man replies. "They'd like you more. Your peers. If you didn't always have to draw attention to yourself. If you could just leave things alone. You've just got on this afternoon," he continues. "You've worked quietly. You can make too many demands on people. People don't like demands being made of them.

"Look at Philip. Look at the way he is. He's always looking out for other people, looking at how to include them. And this afternoon? Well, Peter Pan, you just got on, and look what you did."

And he looks at his work, surprised, excited even, by the painting he has replicated. He grabs his bag and runs up the stairs into the school hall, past the notice-boards, and he feels alight, burning with promise. The main doors bang behind him as he runs down the steps to his father in the waiting car.

Yet, he knows that were he asked to sit outside and turn the abbey into the kind of cloaked, black crow John Piper sees he would not know where to begin. He knows how to paint to satisfy Mr. Miller, but he does not know how to paint for himself.

Chapter 17

He is not clear why his father continues to pay Malcolm if Malcolm is breaking the law. Sometimes his father will play out a scene for the children. He will drop Malcolm in town, after a morning's work, and say, "I'm afraid I haven't got any cash. Can I give you a check?" Malcolm tells him he'd rather have cash, that he can wait while his father gets some money. His father will then be forced to drive round town to find a cashpoint.

When Malcolm has got out of the car, their father turns to them in triumph.

"See!" he tells the children. "Malcolm cannot accept a check as then the authorities would want to know where it came from, and he'd have to admit he is working odd jobs on the side!"

But his father gains nothing by his victory. In fact, all it does is highlight his own complicity in the deception.

The son thinks there are better reasons to dislike

Malcolm: the fact that he was accused of helping himself to money from the church collection, or that one day he threatened to clip his sister round the ear. However, nothing has been said to Malcolm about this.

When pressed, their parents agree that, were Malcolm to strike either of them, he would be dismissed immediately. But when asked what will happen as a result of his having threatened their daughter, they both clam up. They must wait until he actually strikes either one of them.

He wants to say that his parents are setting too high a bar. In this way Malcolm will never be found out and, as a result, Malcolm will never be fired. He reckons this is all his parents ever want—to play at being right without the bother of having to do anything about it.

He knows from his mother that men can be dangerous. She tells stories from her own childhood of strange men and kidnappings that give him a perverse thrill.

"One day, a car followed us all the way back to the boarding house," she tells them. "We were walking back from the village shop, when a black car—sleek black, almost as long as a hearse—pulled level with us. It crept alongside me and my friend Sarah the whole way. A man in a suit was in the driving seat and eventually he leaned over and wound down the passenger window, as though asking for directions, you know? So we stopped to see what he wanted, but he didn't say anything. And the nearside door just swung open. Swung open, like that," and she swings her arm out violently by her side. "And there, crouched up in the passenger footwell, was another man, curled into a ball, as though ready to leap out. After that, we ran all the way back."

She pauses.

"There were always strange men about, in those days. Strange men in cars, down from the city."

He does not think to ask how she knows where they were from.

Why is his mother's world full of these men? he wonders. They must be the product of her overactive imagination, like the spirits she claims to see while walking along the riverbank, or the dragons she believes are to be found on the Malvern Hills. She cannot be allowed to simply walk down a street; there must be some man in a greatcoat following her.

She always tells these stories against herself—they are designed to amuse and illustrate her own naivety. The only exception is the time she confides to him and his sister that, before she married their father, she'd been advised to leave London owing to a stalker. The man called her parents' house once and her mother had answered the phone, told her he sounded nice, that she could do a lot worse. But she remains frightened by the thought of him to this day.

But then, if his mother is not merely being grandiose, if there is some truth to her stories, then it must be that she has done something to deserve it. What can she have done, he wonders; what small, imperceptible gesture—imperceptible even to herself—has she made that gives these men encouragement? Is there some way in which she desires this kind of attention? Suggests their violent advances are welcome?

These vividly painted stories give him nightmares—dreams of men he can only see from the waist down, in trousers and shoes proffering a bag of sweets; or a car, not unlike their own, that screams up to the curb, with the door that swings open to reveal the man crouched down inside. The tremor at these stories comes from their threat, and the realization that there was no one there to protect his mother. How then are he and his sister to stay safe? Who will protect them?

As they grow older, however, the advice from their parents is more obviously directed to his sister. It is she who is implored never to go cycling on her own, it is she who is admonished for telling a strange car which way to take for the neighboring village, it is she who must go with him if they are to walk across the fields.

And yet, he feels sure that he is in need of his sister's protection far more than she is in need of his. Of the two of them, she will put up the greater fight, she is tougher than him.

As if to demonstrate this, he and the landlord of the pub have a secret. For evenings when his father is sat at a table and the boy is sat at the bar, the landlord will join the conversation by standing behind his bar-stool, before resting his hand in the small of the boy's back. It starts so innocently, just a placement, so that the boy does nothing. The hand must merely be there by mistake. But as the weeks go by, the hand becomes bolder. It strokes his buttocks down to the seat and even curls up over his thigh. He worries it will eventually explore the area between his legs.

However, he likes the landlord because he always takes his side in disputes with his father. When the others frown or set their jaws, it is the landlord who nods in his direction and says, "Listen to your son, he knows what he's talking about."

These touches are out of sight of everyone else—they must be, for no one says anything. Not even his father, nor Gillespie, propped on the bar-stool opposite, as high as his twisted spine will allow. He is not quite sure how or why, but he presumes this behavior to be his fault in some way. If he were normal, less prone to standing out, then these sorts of thing would not happen to him.

He is sure this would not happen to the other boys. It would not even happen to his sister. When the boys discuss strange men, it is always the graphic violence they would do to anyone who interfered with them. They'd kick them in the balls. No, Philip and the other boys would not allow such a thing to happen to them.

Why can he not speak with such clarity, such certainty? He wants to remain on friendly terms with the landlord without having to endure his caress. Yet he does not know how to achieve this. For the truth is, while he may resent it, and dislikes the landlord's touches, he likes the landlord, likes that he takes his side, and, on some level, can comfort himself that the unwelcome touches make him special.

Eventually he tells his parents.

"I wish Clive wouldn't keep touching my bottom," he tells them.

His parents are taken aback. What does he mean? He must be mistaken. The landlord has probably only misplaced something; he probably thinks he's resting his hand on the chair.

"No," he insists. "He keeps doing it. And he strokes my bottom. I think you should say something."

Now his parents become quite different.

"Oh, we couldn't possibly," they say.

"That would be frightfully embarrassing," his father says. "You can't accuse a man of that."

"I thought you liked the pub?" adds his mother.

He assures them he does. But when he protests again his father says, "Well, if it's bothering you, you can just ask him not to touch your bottom."

He knows this to be no solution at all. Worse than the landlord's caress is the response he imagines from the room as he pipes up, in the unbroken voice mimicked by Mr. Miller, "Can you stop touching my bottom, please!"

A few weeks later, while his father is at the bar, Clive stands next to him and his father shoots up like he's been hit by an electric current.

"Touch me there again and you'll have to marry me!" his father says, waving his hands around like Eric Morecambe.

Gillespie laughs nervously while the landlord looks a little surprised, but it seems no one knows what his father is on about.

The moment is humiliating. He does not believe the landlord has got close enough to touch his father in the way he touches him; this whole scene is a fabrication, for his benefit. But he will not repeat his father's performance because it was so patently absurd. And so he is resigned to the fact that, because he also likes the pub, because it is where he and his family are happiest together, he must put up with these unwelcome touches. He doesn't dare speak of it to anyone else, for then his ignorance, his lack of worldliness, will be exposed, and that would be the greatest shame of all.

Chapter 18

On the winding road down to the river, among the willow-shade, his mother asks why, if there is a God, he should allow her to be unhappy. He suggests that without unhappiness maybe we could never recognize joy, and she reaches out and takes his hand in hers.

However, he is not convinced by his own argument. For if what he says was true, then why does it not apply equally? While he and his sister must suffer their mother's unhappiness, their friends have ordinary, happy mothers, content to fetch and carry them. That is what he wants—a mother at his beck and call, who loves him, holds him, who will attend to his wants without complaint.

At the pub they turn onto the riverbank, through fields waist-deep in grass. As they trail along the bank, she asks if he can see the spirits, the spirits running between the trees that lean precariously over the river? He tells her he can—that there is something here, something he can feel alive. But no, she insists she means *see,* so he wonders whether he lacks imagination, or an ability to see the things of this world on their other level.

Does she truly have some extra depth of perception? he wonders. He thinks it unlikely. He is disinclined to believe in miracles or mystics because then why are some people favored with such signs or visions and not others?

He is also skeptical owing to how much his mother wants to see these things. How, then, is one to know that it is not a mere fabrication on her part? Like the attention-seeking boy in the year below who claims to break his back every weekend? Maybe she is simply crazy.

Following lunch, she tells them all of a time walking the dogs when she fell to her knees in the dry earth and took up her hands in prayer. Their father simply carries on with the washing up, hands in the sink, soapsuds carelessly splattered around his middle and the crotch of his trousers. He turns to the children as she spins her yarn, giving a smile and wink. In this, his father draws them in against their mother, indicates that he too does not believe her stories. The boy smiles but does not wink back. But he reasons she cannot be mad or his father would not make light of it.

"The dogs sniffed all round me," she says. "I wondered whatever a passerby would have made of it."

Why does she always worry about the good opinion of

others? he thinks. Why is she not solely concerned for his good opinion?

Then again, he wonders what Gillespie would have made of it. While the whole family is cushioned from life's hard edges, Gillespie has seen nature do its worst. This is why they are all in thrall to Gillespie. Gillespie has no time for excess.

When she cries, his father is nowhere to be found. If one of the children fetches him, he will grudgingly drop what he is doing and go to her.

"What's wrong?" he will ask, with little or no conviction. She will sob to be left alone and he'll reply gruffly, "All right then," before giving them a look that says he's done as much as can be reasonably expected.

His father is in error in asking what is wrong, for the children have learned this is not the appropriate question. What she needs is someone to hug her and sit with her. Someone who will stay and dare not leave her alone.

Her absence seeps into every corner of the house, her lack measured in meals missed when she stays in her room or the ticks of the clock as they wait for her to rejoin them. Her tears, her crying, are a signal now. All the while it is clear this is not to be shared. She is ill, she and his father tell friends and neighbors. She is unwell. She has a cold again. She is too tired to come down, to come out, to drop them at school.

When she is back to her old, glorious self, they are

reunited with their mother, and he believes all will be well, it will be fine. But underneath the return to her old self there lies an anxiety that this is not real, this will not last. Just as the long, lush summer days give way to rain and floods in winter, so too this optimism will be washed from beneath their feet.

∞

It is decided he and his sister will stay with respective friends for a few days. He will stay with Philip while she'll stay with Jade.

Philip has a normal family. They have a computer, a games console, and a cabinet that houses a large black television set, with a stereo beneath, all fresh from Radio Rentals.

They do not have a computer or games at home. They only have an old television encased in faux wood, which his father got from a man down the pub.

Philip's room is decorated with football posters and one of Bart Simpson saying "Eat My Shorts," while he has a series of watercolors his parents painted in Cornwall.

They spend the day lying on their bellies on the bedroom carpet, playing computer games. Later they drink squash and cola and roll about on the floor of the living room. After lunch, they walk to the village shop to buy sweets and white candy sticks sold to look like cigarettes. They discuss their impending move to senior school and he realizes Philip is nervous, that he fears this change too.

"You'll be all right," he tells him. "Everybody always likes you."

"So what?" Philip replies.

"Well, if everybody likes you then nothing else matters."

"Why do you need everybody to like you all the time?" Philip challenges him, and he feels this question is about something else, that Philip has hit on something, even as he's offended that anyone could claim a knowledge of him he does not possess himself.

He confides what Mr. Miller advised him, about people liking him more if he made fewer demands, and blushes. So, in the hope of changing the subject, so that the admission might be forgotten, he says again, "You're liked by everybody."

Philip thinks for a minute. "Yes. But I don't care. People can do what they like."

"It's easy for you to say. Easy to say when everyone likes you already."

"I don't think he's right," Philip finally says. "It really doesn't matter. I wish I could get you not to care. I think you're doing just fine." And with that he punches him on the arm.

The boy wonders if this is what friendship is, or love, even. In which you are each just enough for each other, sufficient, and there is nothing to hide or pretend.

In the final hours before bed, they fight and roll across the carpet until they've exhausted themselves, their breath coming hot, their cheeks red as apples. Philip's mother comes in and says it is time for sleep, that it is not the time for getting overexcited. She says it nicely but there is an edge to her voice, something beyond a reprimand.

That night, he sleeps on a mattress on the floor of Philip's room. He feels the difference in height reduces him to the level of a dog or family pet. He is kept awake by the brightness of the moon, which pools in the glass of the window and casts its milky glow across the room's surfaces. He misses his mother. He misses his sister. He even misses his father. He can hear the gentle tick of Philip's sleeping and wishes he were awake. He has never felt so alone, cast adrift in the blue shadow of the moon.

When they come down in the morning, it is to find Philip's older brother, Nick, standing at the kitchen sink. Nick is at boarding school but is on an exeat. He is a year ahead of himself and said to be even cleverer than Philip. He has his back to them as they enter the room; naked to the waist and filling a glass of water. He drains the glass, refills it, and drains it again, and all the while the boy watches the pulse of his Adam's apple, the prick of hair at his chin, and reckons he is so beautiful that, if he ever found a girl like this, this is who he'd marry. When he has finished, Nick sets down the glass and gives the pair of them a wink, before returning to bed. The boy resolves he should wink more; it is charismatic.

Philip also has a normal relationship with his mother. They are cordial—he thanks her and is polite—but every now and again he makes it clear he has a world she is excluded from. Philip is not supplicant to his mother, as he is himself. Unlike Philip, if he's not following his mother about the house, then he is railing at her. Railing at her to leave him alone.

He has rages at home—rages that frighten him and his parents. He is ashamed; he knows he would not get away with this behavior anywhere else, he would not try it on at school. Yet, even as he knows he can't control these moods, he is ashamed his parents should have to suffer them. If he can control himself at school, then he should be able to control himself at home. Yet he resents their love and acceptance, for it is this which allows him to continue to get away with it. It is their love that keeps him bad.

Philip's mother is pretty and friendly. The boy tries— he fears too hard—to be polite and win her over. After lunch he takes his plate through to the kitchen and offers to do the drying up. When she comes upstairs to check on them, asks if they'd like a glass of squash each, he offers to come down and fetch them. She shoos him away from these tasks—all things he would never do at home.

How he behaves at Philip's is how he imagines he should always behave—a good, kind, likable boy. He feels a well of sadness that his parents should have to endure his worst self, for the truth is: he is a tyrant. At home, he ignores his mother's calls for help while expecting to be waited on by his father. Secretly, he reckons he is spoiled and ungrateful. Perhaps if he weren't then things would be better. He helps Philip's mother owing to a desperate sense he should not be found out: she must not know what a selfish, thankless child he is.

When his mother collects him, he hears the doorbell with a combination of dread and relief. He and Philip lie together on the living room sofa and he can hear his mother's voice carrying in. Has he behaved himself? Are you sure? I hope he's been no trouble.

Next to the sound of Philip's mother, his mother sounds so anxious, so keen to be liked. He feels sorry for her and yet hates her at the same time. Her desperation reveals something about her, and in turn about himself.

His sister regularly has friends over, whom she will play with in the garden or shut away in her room. If he tries to join in, he is forbidden. This is his sister's time, his mother says.

He has become more alert to Jade, having been only dimly aware of her before. He notices her browned, athletic legs, her thighs muscled as tree trunks—legs far stronger and browner than his—that flick beneath her gym skirt when she plays netball. When she talks, the corners of her hair catch in her mouth, and he will watch as she pulls strands, wet, from between her lips. He is also fascinated by her neck, longer than other necks— longer than his own, his sister's, the necks of the boys. This extra length exaggerates the small dimple of skin where it meets her collarbone and, from there, on the hot summer days when they are permitted to remove their ties and unbutton their collars, the stretch of skin that runs down beneath her shirt to her developing breasts.

Jade's mother takes her to have her hair tinted in Cressflair and she continues to wear nail varnish in school, although it is forbidden. His sister dresses for Jade and, later, when he searches for them in the house, he cannot find them. He is not meant to go into his sister's room, but pressing his ear to the door he can hear no sound so he pushes it ajar.

Jade is sat in front of the mirror, his sister next to her, bent over, gently applying lipstick to her friend's mouth. The room has a sugary smell like talcum powder. Neither of them has heard him and he finds he is holding his breath, watching as Jade presses her lips tight, releases them, and then tight together again. Only when he moves his foot do they turn and see him, yell at him to get out.

He tries teasing them, but they merely ignore him, choosing earrings and holding them up to one another. Nor are they interested in any of the games he suggests. Instead, they sit together and talk. Their talk is the soft and serious conversation of women. He would like this interaction but it is clear he is not welcome, he is being a nuisance. And even as he knows this, he finds he cannot stop, the air trapped in his throat, a buzzing in his nose. For he'd rather be a nuisance than barred altogether.

Perhaps to placate him, his mother will ask if he'd like someone over. He wishes she would leave things alone. He does not want anyone over. If he wanted anyone over, he'd say. He doesn't mind not having anyone over until his mother asks. And then, by bringing it up, by running through a list of his classmates, all she does is draw attention to his sister's friendships and his lack of them. Her tone is almost pitying. He is alone, alone save for her. By trying to help him find his own way, she merely highlights how encased he is by her.

The truth is, he does not want people over for fear that the oddness in him they already see at school will be compounded by the oddness they find at home. Only his sister is normal and, somehow, this enables her to get away with it in spite of them.

If his mother didn't love him so much then maybe he'd be normal. She loves him too much, with her constant fussing at the school gates with concern as to whether he has packed everything. Her love leaves him feeling guilty, because he knows he is not worthy of it. It lays a claim on him, but it's never as great as the claim he lays on her.

Previously, he has asked whom she loves most—him, his sister, or their father. He knows this to be a trick question, for all mothers love their children best. So, when she says their father—that she is married to their father, which means she must love him more than anybody—he is horrified. He was prepared for her to refuse to pick between him and his sister, but he does not believe she can love his father better than either of them, his father who is so utterly contemptible. It is her duty to choose them over him. Yet, while he is sure she is lying, he cannot explain why she would tell such a lie.

Chapter 19

He is at the dentist's having a tooth capped when the call comes. He does not know why his father has taken him to this appointment, he would have preferred his mother. She was expected to take him but he has not seen her, hearing she was to stay in bed. When his father returns from using the telephone in reception, he gives no explanation, other than to say that his mother has been rushed into hospital and he will be collected by one of the teachers from school.

With the suction pump hanging from the lower left corner of his mouth, the boy cannot speak; he cannot ask why, cannot ask what has happened. If he could, he would beg his father not to leave, or at least not to leave him alone without knowing what is going on. But then perhaps it is just as well he cannot speak, so he does not suffer the indignity of begging.

He does not like the dentist's. His visit today has been

necessitated by catching his left incisor on a chair, while playing "dens" before school. He will be required to stay indoors for the rest of the day. He might even need an anesthetic. It is typical that his parents should be too busy with their own concerns to care about him.

Ten minutes later, he is in the waiting room greeting the geography teacher, a kind man but with a degree of reserve toward the children, one of the younger members of staff, tall and thin, with no shoulders so his body seems to drop straight from his neck, like an Indian runner duck. He would have liked Mr. Miller or some other person. Instead, he will return to school in this young man's red Fiesta, a color so bright it could be a joke.

Everyone is very reticent: the teacher in the car, his form teacher, the school secretary. While he sits out break in the school library, the secretary comes and asks if he wants any biscuits. She is a large, busty woman with the air of someone who feels her job could be done competently if only the school were devoid of children. So this kindness is both unusual and out of proportion; it must be due to what has happened to his mother. It is outrageous anyone should know what has happened to her when he does not. If anyone should know about her, then it is him and his sister.

He finds his sister in the lunch queue and, together, they go to demand news from the secretary. However, having marched into her office, barely stopping for a response to his knock on the door, he is met by a wall of refusal. She is so firm, so resolute and uncaring, he feels as if they are in some secret struggle with one another. There is no news, she tells them. Their father will tell them more when he collects them.

When will their father collect them? To their surprise, it will be at the usual time, at the end of the day. This is not what he expected, this does not seem fair. He has just had his tooth capped. If their mother is in hospital then they should not be in school. But without allowing for any argument or explanation she turns from them to the ringing telephone and says, "You can see I'm very busy."

Their mother has had a reaction to her pills; that is what their father tells them in the car, the air sickly sweet with the smell of his breath. It was not clear to her that the antidepressant she was on would react with paracetamol. The hospital is very nice, he reassures them. Not like a hospital, in fact, more like a hotel.

He does not see why no one will tell them what is really going on. Does his father really imagine him to be both such a child and so stupid? He also feels their being together when the call came, his being abandoned at the dentist's, gives him extra rights in the matter. Finally, it occurs to him that his father has not asked how he got on, not even to see his tooth.

That evening, he and his sister discuss whether they believe their parents' story. He had expected her to believe whatever she was told, so is surprised when it is she who proffers that their mother may have done it deliberately. But when the words are uttered, neither of them knows what to do with them, so they hang awkwardly between them, there yet untouchable. All he can think is how to ensure she never does it again.

Any claim his parents have to authority now strikes him as dubious at best. If his mother were to die, then they would be all alone. They cannot rely on their father. Without his mother, he would have to stand up to his father and finally proclaim himself the man of the house.

☙

In readiness for her return from the hospital, the boy tidies up, scrubs the floors, wipes down and polishes the dining table. Were he to have more time, then he might repaint the house, making it spick and span, replace the beige with warm, rich colors. If the front room had a roaring fire, deep red walls, then the space would feel warm and cozy, like another house in which the people were happy and content.

He resents having to do these chores, just because his father is too oafish to have paid heed to the many times his mother complained that the mess depressed her. It should be his father who breaks his back carrying a slopping mop bucket around the house and the hoover up the stairs.

Instead, the boy scrubs the floor on bony knees, his

hands white with cold. All the while the radio plays and a bottle of wine stands open on the worktop, as his father tramps mud back and forth between the kitchen and garden outside.

"Get out! Get off my floor!" the boy shouts. "Don't you care that it should be tidy when she comes home?" He recognizes his words are those of a housewife and hates this fact, all while his father continues on through the house, step after muddy step.

Over the following days and weeks, he and his sister form an alliance. It is hot out, but they put the fan heater on in the sitting room and watch and rewatch old videos bought from the supermarket bargain bin. When their father looks in on them, he complains the room is like an oven. If they're cold, why don't they go and run around outside? But they simply laugh at him as he closes the door.

They decide to confront their father. He is out in the garden, shears in hand, trimming the corner of the beech hedge. They haven't prearranged it, but he and his sister ask their questions in turn.

"She wasn't herself then," his father tells them, barely pausing his work.

What if, the boy fears, the truth is that that was when she was most like herself? What if she meant to do it? The closest he can get is to ask, "What if she was herself?"

"She may have meant to do it in the moment," his father replies against the snap of the shears, "but that is why she can't have been herself." Beech leaves drop to the ground.

"What does that mean?" his sister asks.

"She only did it then because she was not herself. And now she is feeling better." And with that he grabs the broom standing nearby and begins to sweep up the pile of fallen leaves.

What he and his sister do not understand is why, having taken all the pills, she walked down to the river and waded in, only to walk back home, soaked through?

When their mother returns home, she asks if they know the painting of Ophelia by Millais, before fetching a large art book and placing it in front of them on the kitchen table. She turns to an image of a woman, lying as though asleep in a bath. The water of the stream is clear, the grass and reeds burst with green and, floating next to her, just out of reach of her thin fingers, lies a rose.

"I wanted to lie like that," his mother says. "But then it occurred to me it wouldn't be like that at all. The water was cold and dirty. Instead I'd have been pale, my face all bloated like a body in some detective drama. So I got out and walked home."

What surprises him in this story isn't his mother's madness but her stupidity. Why did she want to die like in a painting? Doesn't she know the difference between life and make-believe? Why was it only by lying in the river that this became evident to her?

Later, finding her in bed upstairs, he asks her: "Why did you do it?"

"I don't know," she says. Her face is wistful and the sun outside spills across the counterpane, catches the gray in her hair. "Sometimes there isn't a reason, or we don't know why we do things."

He cannot believe this and nor does it satisfy him as an answer.

Chapter 20

Three summers ago, a farmer in the neighboring village shot himself. His wife called him in for supper at the end of a long day hay cutting, only for the man to fetch his shotgun and blow his face away in the orchard. Of their two children, it was the son who heard the shot and ran out to find him.

He knows all this because the men at the pub discussed it. But now, if he hears this family's name drift down the long corridor when he arrives with his father, the voices drop silent as soon as they enter the bar.

The children also used to go to his school. Following their father's death, they were allowed to leave lessons unannounced to go and speak with Mrs. Edelman. Mrs. Edelman dresses in long skirts and chunky amber jewelry and would come into the school especially. To see Mrs. Edelman, and having her sent for, is a privilege. Everyone wants an excuse to see Mrs. Edelman. With her power to pull people out of class she has demonstrated she is bigger than the school. He would like to speak with this woman but, because their mother is alive, he cannot.

There is no connection between him and the farmer's children for he has a terrible secret: he envies them. How much easier it would be if his mother were dead. If she were dead there would be an end to it. One night, as he lies awake and balls the edges of the duvet tight round his neck, he holds his breath and strains for a sign of her in the silence. Flies thrum in the dark. Can he hear her crying, he wonders, or is it merely the wail of wind coming down the chimney?

He does not know what he is to do. He does not want to have to get up, to go and comfort her, nor does he want her to do it next door, while he is here. He does not want to see the mess, to be confronted with it. He cannot manage this never knowing. He would like it all to be taken care of—for her to be neatly packaged up and taken away, like a parcel, so he can be left to get on with his life.

He can never utter these thoughts aloud for they are wicked. To speak them is all that is required to make them reality. Then he will have killed his mother. So no, he keeps this to himself, along with how he hates his own mother, hates her for the power she wields over them, hates her enough to wish she had had the courage to go through with it. Then he could speak with

Mrs. Edelman, then everyone would know just how much he has had to put up with. He knows these are not the thoughts of a loving son, they are the thoughts of a monster.

The next morning, when he sees his mother and she hugs him, gets him ready for school, he remembers them and is overcome with remorse. What makes it worse is he is sure his mother is trying to make it up to him. She asks if he'd like anything from the shops, or something special when he gets home for tea. He snaps at her by way of reply. He can never truly say what he wants to say—that he hates how the specter of her death has won her a silent victory over all the house.

If he and his sister daren't upset their mother, for fear of the consequences, that means the only person they can take things out on is their father. His car leaves earlier each morning and is gone for longer each trip. Throughout the day, he will make a play of things he has forgotten in town, requiring further journeys, on which he is gone for hours at a time. His breath smells when he returns, his movements are that little more uncertain. Yet he still collects them from school, gets the supper on, before driving down to the pub in the evening.

What the boy cannot deny is that his sense of the family has changed. It is nothing so dramatic as a shift in allegiance, for he cannot ever imagine being servile to a man so useless as his father, but nor is he prepared to accept his mother's dominion over the house any longer.

When she gets up again, his mother will complain to them about their father. Yet, while he agrees his father is impossible, he will not have it. Now she is better, she floats about the house, wrapped in a silk scarf with long dangly earrings, playing the part of a brisk mother who is disapproving and ready to reassert control. But she has no authority here. No one mentions the days, the weeks she has spent in bed, the curtains drawn, the cold mugs of coffee with dark, caramel rims inside.

The weekend of the village hall barbecue, his father offers to help set up and is gone for most of the afternoon. When the son walks over the fields to speak with him, dry yellow grass pricks at his bare legs. He can feel the pulse of blood in his temples and fences swim in the heat haze off the ground. His father is busy with the other men, all drinking from a beer keg while they work. As he mops his brow his face flames red against the white of his handkerchief.

When he returns later, his father appears ill and says he will have an early night. Even as their mother furiously ushers him to their room, she explains to the children, "We have to tell people he has heat stroke."

It seems to the boy that all those who worked with him on setting up the barbecue will know this to be a lie. Yet they must tell everyone the lie, and everyone will say how awful it is, thereby lying in turn.

It is evident that the only person capable of looking after the family and restoring order is himself. And yet, there are moments he sees himself as though from a long way away, hovering far above the family home, like a kestrel above the hedgerows, and feels despairingly small: a little boy wanting to scream, "Won't anyone look after me?"

Chapter 21

Their whole year group is in the art room. It is hot out but cool underground and a breeze comes in from the open window off the fire escape. The sun lays a broad bar of light across the tables. It darkens and then brightens as clouds pass over, as though a light is being turned on and off.

He and Philip work beside each other, set apart from the others. Drawing on large sketch boards, they reproduce rooflines from a photograph while Mr. Miller shuttles between them, occasionally taking a pencil to reorient an angle or block a wall into place.

The rest of the class works on while a battered radio buzzes with tinny pop. There is the low-level odor of pubescent sweat mixed with over-applied deodorant. The teacher moves to stand between two girls, making a pretense of checking their work.

"Yes, yes," he nods, before making a single flourish with a paintbrush.

Are they dating? Mr. Miller suddenly asks the class. Do any of the boys in their year have girlfriends?

The boy is used to this line of questioning. One of his aunts regularly calls up and, if he answers the phone, says, "Oh gosh! Is your voice breaking? Or do you just have a cold?" She will then proceed to tell him that his cousin, her son, George's voice has broken. He will feel a flutter that maybe his voice has broken without his noticing, while suspecting that he is merely tired. The next time she calls she will be sure to say, "Yes, I think you must have had a cold last time. Are you dating anyone? George has a delightful new girlfriend—"

So he is used to these sorts of questions—questions designed to humiliate.

Of the entire class, it is to Morrow, with his broken voice and need for a razor, that Mr. Miller chiefly seems to address himself. Does he have a girlfriend? Is there someone he likes?

The boy knows that there is someone Philip likes. Philip asked his help to write a love poem. He did not know why Philip should need his help, but Philip told him it was because of his marks in English. While he was gratified Philip should think him equipped with the eloquence required of a lover, he does not believe this to be the reason.

He does not want to hear of Philip's desire, or those of others; it lowers them in his estimation. Nor does he want to share his own desire. For others to know of his desire is like exposing a wound to the open air. No, he knows from when some boys got hold of his liking for Jade that it had a currency he hadn't anticipated. He had revealed something, something not evident to himself. That is what their chants said, parroting it around, that they had something over him.

He fears he does not meet the standard of a lover—that he is too frigid for that.

The class turns the conversation around—Does Mr. Miller have a girlfriend? Has he ever been married? Why has he never married?

As far as they know, all the masters are married. Some of their wives teach in the pre-prep and those that don't appear on speech day, at the end of the school year. He remembers meeting the history master's wife, on the school lawn last year. She had offered him a slice of cake, before taking him aside and saying she understood from her husband that he was a very clever boy. What did he plan to do? she asked. He has hoped to see her ever since.

They know Mr. Miller is not married. No wife appears on speech day. It has never been asked about, never been raised.

"I did propose to someone once," he grudgingly admits, working on his own drawing now, scratching out lines and not raising his eyes from the paper to the expectant faces of the girls and boys.

"And what did she say? What did she say?" they chorus.

"She said no." He pulls a face before adding, "She turned me down."

In the awkward silence that follows, silent but for the itch of the pencil against the cartridge paper, the class begins to laugh. He doesn't know who starts it—perhaps it is him. But their laughter fills the gap, the silence, for there is a heavy air in the room and the sound of something crackling beneath the convulsive back and forth of the teacher's shading.

It seems Mr. Miller joins in, before suddenly turning to Morrow.

"You will have no problem getting a girlfriend," he pronounces.

Morrow does not seem surprised, nor gratified even, as the boy would be himself. The remark does not even register—the fact so evident to Morrow already.

"Nor will you," he says to Philip, standing tall, looking each of them in the eye in turn. "But as for you," turning to the boy, speaking with a measured tone, "it will not be easy for you. You will always struggle."

He feels crushed. He knows this to be true. The gentle titter carrying about the room only confirms it, although there is something uncertain behind it, restrained.

Mr. Miller is no longer drawing and the pencil rests

between his fingers, yet he feels he can still hear the grind of the lead against paper, feel its point being rubbed away. An air of light triumph rises off Morrow, and Philip next to him.

"Why?" he demands. Of course it must be true, for Mr. Miller has said it. But he must know why.

"It's all about S.A.," the master says cryptically, his loosely gripped pencil returning to the paper. But when they ask what he means, what S.A. stands for, he clams up. "I have said too much already," he says, shrugging and throwing a hand over his shoulder with a half-smile.

It is only as the class fires off a series of guesses, each increasingly improbable, before getting stuck on South Africa, that the teacher relents.

"Sex appeal," he tells them. "It is all about sex appeal."

And there it is. Named. Set down. Yes, as if he'd always known. Is this it, the indissoluble difference between himself and Philip? Perhaps there really is a quality, a quality that is quantifiable—one Philip has in abundance—a quality that determines, quite literally, the ability for you to be loved.

It occurs to him that what Jade and Philip share is not goodness, not even beauty, but something else. A brightness, a lightness; like some secret knowledge he needs to possess. Whatever this quality is, he is susceptible to it. It provokes a need in him to be physically close to them, to be in their company, simply to hear the hushed sound of them whispering into his ear, maybe even to touch them—anything to keep the urgent sensation alive.

As they all file out of the art room at the end of class, Mr. Miller reaches out a hand and grips Philip's arm. The pair of them bow their heads together and there follows an exchange of voices, quiet and indistinguishable. Philip's back is to the boy, and it looks as though the teacher has something in his hand, but the moment is very brief, and as Philip moves off again he sees the man's hands are empty.

"This doesn't concern you," the master calls over.

Philip joins him and he asks, "What was that about? What did he give you?"

But Philip is dismissive, even slightly embarrassed. "Nothing. Just leave it."

"But he gave you something, didn't he? What was it?"

"Leave me alone, Danny. And stop clinging to me like some little girl."

The master has named his want of something and now he fears Philip sees it as well. He feels Philip drawing a line between them, as though his friend has entered a room, only to stand in the doorway and tell him not to follow. And if Philip can see it—if it is plain to him—perhaps it is legible to everyone else too?

Chapter 22

M r. Miller edits the school magazine, *Inklings*, which comes out every summer term. Pulling together the best written work produced in the school, be they poems, short stories or even the odd essay, it is printed on sheets of A4, folded and bound in cream card, and held together with two staples. Being published is the highest honor the boy can conceive of, greater even than having artwork chosen for the school noticeboards. But he does not share this, for he recognizes that none of the other children cares as he does.

He is therefore deeply gratified when Mr. Miller asks if he'd mind helping. He will be something like assistant editor. Will he get paid? the boy asks. Or be named as editor in the inside cover? No, Mr. Miller replies, the glory will be a private one. He readily accepts. Not only does the role of editor confer importance upon him but it will also enable him to spend more time with Mr. Miller. Maybe it will show he is not ill-favored after all.

He is not prepared for the amount of work involved. It seems being assistant editor requires him to type all the work into the library computer. He does not mind this—being given permission to use the school's one Apple Macintosh is an honor, made all the more enjoyable by the satisfying click on and off of the caps lock key. All the same, he is forced to use his morning and lunch breaks to get the work done, until Mr. Miller relents and allows him to spend a double English class on the project too.

He had imagined that by being assistant editor this might result in more of his own work being favored, but this is not the case. If anything, his own contribution is meager in comparison with past editions. Instead, he must type up the work of others in his year, and those who have particularly excelled in the years below, before saving it all in ClarisWorks. One is a piece by his sister about the visit of their aunt, which he does not believe to be good.

Prior to each of these sessions, he must go to the English room and collect the latest pile of compositions selected, corrected, and edited down for inclusion by Mr. Miller. However, today, there is no pile. He searches for Mr. Miller and finds him outside the school hall. Is his job done? Are all the pieces typed up now? But no, there is still one batch left, although he has left these at home. He retrieves a set of keys from his jacket pocket.

"I am taking a session in the nets this afternoon. You know where my house is, this is the key for the front door. Run along and fetch the manuscripts on the kitchen table, won't you? It is the first room you will come to."

He holds a brass key by the tip, between thumb and forefinger, and the others revolve gently beneath his hand.

If ever there were a sign of his importance, being handed the keys to the master's house trumps any editorship, named or otherwise. More than the offer of his keys, the casualness of the gesture is what strikes the boy. He is being given the keys as though the house were his own, or somewhere he went all the time. His father would never trust him the way Mr. Miller does.

"Hurry back!" the teacher tells him. "I'll need the keys. I'll be in the nets."

Mr. Miller lives in a small house, almost directly opposite the school. The boy reckons a terrace—smaller than their family home—ill-befitting of a man so superior to his father.

It is baking hot outside and the cars flash like knives as he crosses Church Street. By comparison, the alley, which leads to the master's front door, is cool with shade and the walls are drawn with dark green lines beneath the guttering. Inside, he finds the kitchen, somewhat untidy, with a radio on the table and a paper open at the sports results. Next to them is a plate with crumbs and a knife edged with butter. But there are no manuscripts here.

Into the next room, he can see a desk stacked with books and a mess of papers; hardbacks minus their dust jackets, with bleached and faded leaves. Is he to go in? Recently he incurred the master's wrath for coming back to the art room having been unable to find a pile of new sketchbooks, another time for bringing the wrong text-books to class. So no, he will not go back to the school for further instruction when he might use his own initiative.

This other room is carpeted, the ceiling low. There is an old runner that leads to a single stair, which must twist and turn to the staircase. The walls are partially hidden behind a series of bookcases, waist height, full of books with some volumes turned on their side, resting on top of others.

He could live here, he thinks. Mr. Miller has real art: paintings like those they imitate in the art room, not the dark, Edwardian prints of cathedral closes favored by his father. How much better suited he would be to a home like this, full of books and art, and a radio tuned to the cricket, rather than repeated broadcasts of the news, with its incremental changes.

He approaches the desk, on top of which sits a small, white statue of a semi-nude boy, blowing pipes. Next to it is a book of detective fiction, like some paltry Agatha

Christie, and he is surprised as he cannot imagine *Death in Venice* being to the man's taste.

Then, on a foldout workspace he finds what he has come for: a series of five compositions, all in varying scrawls. The only commonality is the red ink of Mr. Miller's tall, looping script in the margins. But, as he grabs them, a different pile of papers crashes to the floor. He hurriedly gathers them up and replaces them, but from among the pile falls a clean, fresh envelope. "Philip," he reads in Mr. Miller's hand, only in unfamiliar blue.

The flap is open but there is nothing inside. But this does not matter—it is already enough that Mr. Miller should have written an envelope with Philip's name on it. He thinks back to the art room, to the teacher's grabbing of Philip's arm on his way out of the room. He is overcome with a bitter disappointment, so strong he could wish them dead. Yet which of them should be the object of his rage he does not know.

He considers rifling through the papers but cannot bring himself to stoop so low. If Philip is to receive something extra, something special, then he must too. However, he will not demean himself by ensuring that this is so. He will wait for whatever it is to be awarded and only then will he challenge the unfairness if he is not acknowledged at the same time.

And yet, neither can he bring himself to pick up the envelope, as though doing so would be to go too far. So no, he leaves it where it is on the floor and grabs the five manuscripts.

Back in the street, the abbey bells chime and the choristers line up to process for evensong. He runs into the school, into the front hall, which, with the cold of the flagstones, feels damp in comparison to the heat of the day outside. And there is Mr. Miller, his shirt-sleeves rolled up, preparing to put on his jacket and sweep out and join the choristers.

"Ah, Peter Pan!" he exclaims, taking the keys. "You get the manuscripts? Excellent! More Puck than Peter," the man adds. "The boy can fly the world in forty minutes!" He opens the door, blinding them with the sun of late afternoon and, with that, he is gone.

Chapter 23

M r. Miller and Mrs. Walters are to be thrown to-gether to direct the school play, a play Mr. Miller has written himself. Mrs. Walters is his old form teacher. If she sometimes told him off for talking over her, for showing off, for shouting out the answer when one of his classmates struggled to summon it, it was only what he deserved. So when he learns they are to work together he is pleased.

However, as the rehearsals progress it is clear all is not well. The pair of them disagree, openly, in front of the children. Mrs. Walters is sent on errands, the sort given only to a subordinate. Can she get coffee; photo-copy additional scripts; sit at the back to check whether the cast is audible? All the while, Mr. Miller stands at the front, moving the children about like chess pieces.

Mr. Miller confides to him in the art room that the woman is impossible. Her suggestions, her interpretations, are absurd. The boy can only agree, for his path is set, his alliance made. While he loves Mrs. Walters, he cannot bring himself to defend her for she is of the past. The form teachers in the prep school are all men, while their counterparts in the pre-prep, like Mrs. Walters, are all women. It is clear they are to perform a different function: the women are there to be kind; the men are there to prepare them for senior school exams. The world of adults is the world of men; to set aside childish things means setting aside Mrs. Walters.

Yet he remains uncomfortable. Over dinner at home, he wonders aloud why Mr. Miller should treat her this way—perhaps her ideas really are very stupid, he offers. Or maybe she interferes. After all it is his play.

His parents do not offer any interpretation of their own.

He thinks no more of it until a couple of days later, when he is in the art room with the whole of his year. In the middle of an explanation of perspective, Mr. Miller calmly gestures in his direction and tells the class they cannot trust him. He will only run home and tell his parents.

The boy can't make out what he is on about—what is it he could have done?

"You cannot trust him. He will only tell tales on you. And I wouldn't lend him anything or leave him with it, either. He will only rifle through your things."

He goes on, "You are nothing but a sneak, a mummy's

boy. You are too much, with your histrionics and your relentless performance. Running off telling tales to your father when he is no longer headmaster, getting me in trouble."

It is only then he sees what must have happened. His father has raised with the headmaster the teacher's complaints about Mrs. Walters at one of their monthly governors' meetings.

He cannot understand why his father has interfered. Now Mr. Miller is furious with him, just like he was over *The Hay Wain.*

Then, just as suddenly, with a different, more concerned tone, Mr. Miller changes tack and tells the boy that he ought to go to boarding school. He somehow feels caught in a performance, to which this is the crescendo. He does not want to go to boarding school, he replies— although he cannot say why: that at boarding school he would be made to fag like Tom Brown, would be bullied. Worst of all, that he will be away from his parents.

Faced with no reasoned argument, the master says that he must go to boarding school, to escape the silliness of home. He is not sure what this can mean, although fears he does—that what the master calls the silliness of home is exactly what he is desperate to cling to: that only a baby would cling to his mother's dresses, a mother who falls for his lies and lets him off school; only a baby would want to stay at home to be waited on by his parents, parents who spoil and indulge him; only a baby would prefer to be smothered at home over striking out in the world—essentially, a home that is his dominion, one over which he rules in a manner utterly unbefitting a child.

But no, if the master does mean this then he does not say so. Instead, he challenges him, "Do you think you will survive at senior school? Do you? Well, you will see what's coming to you! You will discover your place, your status in the world. They'll see you for what you are."

After class, Mr. Miller takes him to one side. He leans into him, his lips so close to his left ear they almost brush it.

"Did you go through my things?" he asks, quietly. "When you so kindly went to my house, I wondered whether you hadn't taken the chance to do a bit of snooping?"

The word "kindly" has a gross edge, a nastiness far removed from its meaning.

The boy can feel the prick of tears in his eyes and swallows them down.

"No," he replies. "No," he says again.

The man makes a gesture for him to go but then, as though thinking better of it, touches his sleeve.

"Do you know why you need to go to boarding school? It is because your father is a drunk, a lush, an alcoholic. He's the joke of the town. While your mother is crazy, like a southern belle in some ghastly American play!

Why on earth would you want to stay at home, you stupid boy?"

He pauses before going on. "I also worry you are not a suitable friend for Philip, you know," he says. "That boy could be sullied by his acquaintance with you. You are an utterly unsuitable, corrupting friend for a boy like him. That is all."

He throws his hand up in a loose gesture of dismissal.

At home, he cannot tell his parents what Mr. Miller has said for the shame is too deep. He cannot tell them because it will reveal that he sees through them, that he heard all this and said nothing. He did nothing to defend either himself or them because he knows it all to be true.

Chapter 24

The boys in his year are getting changed from extra swimming. It is late afternoon and the sun beats down from a cloudless sky. The gates are locked, the school is deserted so it feels like the start of the holidays, when afternoon rolls into evening and on into an expanse of summer, when the usual rules do not apply.

He takes in the heights of the other boys, the hairs on their legs. One even has a puff of hair above the waistband of his trunks. He does not want his own, clean body sullied with hair. Yet, he has to admit, there is something about the boys and girls on the cusp of adulthood, those boys with their broad, developed shoulders and swarthy skin. Stepping from the tendrils of his trunks onto the cold, tiled floor, his body is childish in comparison.

He is acutely aware of his own body. The other week the school photograph was taken and, as every year, when they lined up by year group, he was shuffled down to stand with boys two years his junior. They gloat, these boys: his presence at once elevates them while reducing himself. He does not believe the school should sanction such humiliation. Why should they be ordered by height when the teachers are not?

When he, Philip and Morrow are the only ones left, Morrow goes to shower while Philip dries himself, running a towel back and forth over his back. The boy finds he cannot take his eyes from the sway of the newly adult penis emerging from the thicket of hair at Philip's groin. Oblivious to the fact of his own staring, he watches it swell and grow to stand in a series of hesitant, incremental movements, before the top unfurls like a bud on a stem.

He has seen Philip watching him, they have been observing each other while never once meeting one another's eye. Philip looks strangely confused—not embarrassed so much as unsure of himself. It is only when he meets Philip's gaze that there is a change: an awareness, where there had been none before, that he is doing something forbidden.

Philip opens his towel out wide behind his back, as though baring his erection, then smiles—a terrible, knowing smile—before neatly wrapping himself away.

Neither of them says anything when Morrow returns from the shower. Yet he feels sure Philip will tell Morrow, and he can't imagine Morrow would understand—

Morrow has no need to measure himself against others, no anxiety about being found wanting in comparison.

The three of them dress in silence. But when he goes to retrieve his bag from a corner of the changing room, he returns to find Philip whispering something in Morrow's ear. The pair of them look at him and smile but say nothing as they file out. He is last to leave and ensures the changing room door is closed behind him.

Outside, a lawnmower wars with the sounds of kids kicking a football against the playground wall. Philip places his arm around Morrow's shoulders in a gesture at once intimate but also adult, manly. *He* would not feel comfortable putting his arm around Morrow like this. The pair of them huddle together as they walk, their backs to him, and for a brief moment he thinks he sees that awful smile again before they slowly walk away.

Chapter 25

The boy speaks to his parents. He cannot bear to be in the same room as the master, he particularly does not want to be alone with him. He cannot say why. It is not as if he touched him somewhere; it is worse. Maybe it would have been better if he had. For fear of hurting them, as well as humiliating himself, he cannot tell them what Mr. Miller said about them for he will have to acknowledge his failure to defend them. Nor can he mention what the man said about his lack of sex appeal because such an observation is shameful, and all the more so because it is true. No, all he can say is that Mr. Miller teased him in front of the other children, mimicked his voice, and ridiculed his liking of Constable.

His parents are not overly bothered. Perhaps he has been irritating in his remonstrations with the master, they suggest. Or about his liking for *The Hay Wain*? Perhaps he needles him by trying to ingratiate himself to such an extent? But no, he insists, the man is a monster, a tyrant, and he does not wish to attend his lessons anymore.

What the boy can't convey is the injustice of being passed over. Whereas before he was a favorite, now he is an object of ridicule. It is surely far worse than if he'd never been favored at all.

His mother will speak with the headmaster. His father will not, his father says Mr. Miller is the best tenor the school has ever had. He is not prepared to kick up a fuss about some teasing over artworks. She will go into school to complain alone.

He knows his mother loves him. While he waits at home, she will go into battle for him, explain that he cannot attend the master's lessons anymore. She dresses in a tweed skirt and jacket, puts on her lipstick. He and his sister know their mother is to be feared in lipstick.

A week later, the school secretary informs him he must go and see the headmaster. The headmaster is a stern, slightly scary man. He has hair that moves all of a piece, brylcreemed to his scalp in a hard side-parting. He has thick-framed glasses, drawn in black felt-tip, and his face is flushed. If he were easy and jocular, the boy might imagine him a drinker, like his father. But he has none of his father's frivolity. He always wears his graduate gown, the sleeves and fold of which flap around his arms, giving the impression of a great crow.

The headmaster also has a glass eye—blue with a

milky texture. Its stillness means his remaining eye always appears restless—darting about. No one knows how the headmaster lost an eye. His mother claims he lost it in the war, but this is just one of her stories. His father scoffs at her suggestion and says he is much too young to have been in the war, it will have merely been some accident.

When the boy thought the headmaster had lost his eye in the war, he felt sorry for him and that he was heroic. An accident or, worse, an illness, confers no such trait. In fact, he feels a blame must attach to the headmaster for this. Just as he bears some responsibility for not being taller, for not being as athletic as his classmates, so too the headmaster must bear some responsibility for losing his eye. Why did he not blink or turn his head away?

He is shown into the headmaster's study where the man asks him to take a seat on one of the gold-covered chairs. He would like to take the armchair, but it is clear this is the headmaster's seat, so he is forced to take a seat on the sofa. However, this is not like any sofa he has seen before: the back is very high, while the seat is very shallow, so he has the sensation of being on the edge of his seat, and being towered over at the same time.

The headmaster gestures to a small round table between them, upon which is a china pot of tea, two cups and saucers, and a small plate of biscuits. These are not the bourbons or custard creams from break, rough and broken from the biscuit tin, but refined, wafer-thin biscuits dusted with sugar. He waits for the headmaster to offer him one but it seems the gesture he made was it—the boy is expected to pour the tea.

"I asked you here today," the headmaster begins, "for something of a man-to-man chat. Do you know what I mean by a man-to-man chat?" He peers at him while the boy pours, the spout of the teapot chattering against the rim of the mug.

"Yes, of course."

"Good, good," he says, reassured. "We have had some complaints about a member of staff—a member of staff I know you have had some problems with—and it seemed to me prudent, sensible, to hear whether you can verify any of the things I have been hearing."

There is a pause. Clearly his mother has done her work.

"I can't tell you what these complaints are, you understand. They are confidential."

He does not understand this—if his is the only complaint, why does the man beat around the bush?

"And you are not to go and tell anyone of our conversation here either. This is between ourselves—man-to-man, you understand?

"Now, the complaint that has been made is about Mr. Miller. I understand you have had extra lessons with him, he is—was—a favorite of yours." The headmaster's hand makes a gesture that indicates how distasteful childish preference is to him. "Are you aware of any instances—conversations, I mean—in which Mr. Miller has been inappropriate? Or made inappropriate suggestions?"

He can think of plenty of instances. Instances in which Mr. Miller has mimicked his voice, mocked him about *The Hay Wain*. Is his appreciation, or lack of it, of John Constable inappropriate?

"Well, he went on about *The Hay Wain*—"

"No, no. Do you know what I mean by inappropriate? I mean where he has said—or done—something"—there is a strained pause during which the boy feels he is perhaps meant to supply the word himself—"sexual," the headmaster finally adds.

How does the headmaster know? Has Mr. Miller joked about his lack of S.A. in the staff room, perhaps? He will not share this humiliating exchange about himself.

The boy is about to speak but the headmaster raises a hand as though to immediately disabuse him of any unwarranted reply. "I don't mean to you, obviously."

The boy flushes at this "obviously." Who can he mean if not himself?

"I mean in relation to any of your classmates. To one in particular. However, I am not at liberty to say whom."

The boy senses he is not doing as expected. He does not have the right answers, the ones required to satisfy the headmaster.

"Are you aware of any letters being written? Anyone being given a letter, or letters, at all?" the headmaster asks.

"No," he blurts out, because there have been no letters, have there? He has received no letter. He knows there was an envelope but there was nothing in it. Nor will he mention the scene in the art room, for he did not see anything pass between them. He will not make more of it than he should, in case the headmaster were to accuse him of merely being jealous.

The headmaster clears his throat. "So you know nothing of this? There is nothing you can add?" he asks, standing and pressing his hands down the front of his trousers.

"No," the boy replies, for he is not a tell-tale. He will not make the same mistake as his injudicious remarks about Mrs. Walters. He can be trusted.

Is that it? he wonders. Have his mother's words amounted to nothing?

As he leaves, he thinks he wants the man fired. He wants him dead. He would destroy him if he could. Somehow, the man has left an indelible mark upon him, like a thumbprint in half-dry clay. He resents this mark upon him. He wants to remove the stain, but what if he cannot? What if the mark is there for always?

༄

Suddenly, the master is no longer there. The headmaster takes his lessons and because he doesn't explain why, only telling the class that he will be teaching them until the end of term, no one dares ask. They open their exercise books and a slow, numb silence hangs in the air as Morrow reads from *Julius Caesar*. They are then asked questions from parts they have not studied, to which none of them can think of answers.

His father tells him Mr. Miller has been dismissed for sending love letters to one of the boys.

"But I didn't get a letter," he interrupts.

"For heaven's sake, Daniel!" his father snaps. "What you have to realize is that it wasn't about you. He was dismissed for sending letters to someone else. It had nothing to do with you. Nothing whatsoever. It wasn't about some paintings."

This is not known by anyone but the school governors—his father has only told him, he says, out of sheer exasperation, to illustrate the fact that the man's dismissal has nothing to do with his own complaints, complaints his father believes are trivial matters of disagreement over Constable.

His father will not tell him whom the letters were sent to, but the boy knows. The art teacher has sent love letters to Philip. That is why he has been dismissed. He recognizes something abnormal about this but at the same time imagines Philip will have been pleased. Surely it is better to have been chosen, better to be wanted than not?

At the end of term, they line up in their year groups

for the prize-giving service in the abbey. The light shines through the high-up windows, down into the transepts and drapes across the nave. He takes a hymn book and looks either side for his parents, hoping they do not notice that he is entering alone.

He picks out the wives of masters, and those boys and girls who left in previous years and have now come back. Those who return are almost never those he wants to see. Nor does he want to have a sense of them gently growing, unobserved, like plants in a greenhouse. He realizes that among the polka-dot faces, he is searching for Mr. Miller—his nose crooked, his brows heavy. But he does not know why—he does not want to see this man, he'd be frightened if he did, of the anger or hatred he might find there. But neither can he cope with him not being there at all, just quietly removed. There is no empty seat for him among the staff, no mention of him in the service. It is as if water has closed over him and left no trace.

Later, among the trestle tables set up on the lawns outside the main school building, the headmaster comes over, a plate with a sandwich in hand, and speaks with his father. The boy does not want to eavesdrop but they are only talking about the top line of the choir anyway. That and who can be found to sing tenor solos, because now they are one short.

Chapter 26

They sit together at a table in the hotel gardens, where they are served by a local boy of about sixteen.

"Aren't we having a lovely holiday?" their mother asks, as she takes a mouthful of scone. "Oh, and the best scones ever. Aren't these simply the best scones you've ever tasted?" she beams, leaning in. "Do you have enough cream, darling? Daddy, what do you think? Isn't this simply the most glorious tea?" and she turns in her chair, as though to check she's been heard behind the counter and maybe even so far as the kitchen.

"I wonder how they all are down the pub," says his father.

"Oh," she begins, stroking down her skirt. "They'll be just the same as normal. It's only been two days," she adds.

"I know. I just can't help wondering what they're all doing. Maybe we should send them a postcard."

And as if seizing hold of this idea, his mother grins at him and his sister and begins, "How do you like the sound of that, children? We must send them a postcard. Would you like that? We can all sign it. I expect they'll put it behind the bar for when we get home."

"I imagine we'll get home first," his father mutters.

"I don't want to send a postcard," the boy mumbles into his tea.

"Oh," says his mother. "Come on. Of course you do."

"No."

"But you're having a nice time, aren't you?"

The boy who serves them has a bracelet of beads around his wrist and a loose white shirt that clings to the contours of his back. He turns to the boy as he sets a sweating bottle of Coke on the table and seems to flash a private smile.

This older boy is alert, with reflex timing and coordination. He has seen him catch a stack of falling dishes, before the cafe owner had even felt her elbow graze them from the counter. He slaps the flat of his palm against the top of his fist and back again when bored, his whole body as taut as a coiled spring, dancing to its own rhythm. He smiles when he speaks with the family, as though playing some sort of joke that he is only about to reveal.

The boy is seized by a knowledge, a certainty, that this older boy is Philip. Not that he looks like him, resembles him, but *is* Philip. That this is who Philip will become, who Philip already is—that they are one and the same. And, as a result, he makes a study of him. He becomes intimately acquainted with the way he moves, his upright posture, the roll of his hips as he swaggers, the thinness of his fingers relative to his thick knuckles and finger joints, the prick of fair hair on his upper lip and chin.

He needs to maintain a constant vigil, ready to suppress anything that might betray him, might confirm Mr. Miller was right. Maybe if he could live with this boy, if they could become friends and share themselves with each other, if only he could put himself into this boy somehow, he could live as this boy lives.

He decides to follow him, as though this boy will show him the way. He hears him say he will finish work and go down to Pentle Bay—the farthest beach, on part of the island isolated but for the heliport. The boy doesn't tell his sister why they are going, only that they will walk the coastal path, round to the Abbey Gardens and onto the bay.

They follow the shoreline up from the hotel to a small castle overlooking the channel, out to another island. They trip the narrow path, between the bracken, their steps muffled by the sandy earth. The walk comes out at an awkward dog-leg to a cafe, backed onto some public toilets and a small wooden outbuilding housing commercial bins. There is the faint stench of food rotting in the baking heat. They buy fruit Polos, not available at home, before his sister returns to the hotel, leaving him to go on alone.

The beach is a curl of sand, like a discarded fingernail, abutted by water on one side and hugged by the tall, long grasses of the dunes on the other. The sea is calm and waves flop onto the shore.

However, when he gets there the older boy is not alone. There is a girl here with him. He can see them from his vantage point up on the rocks, entering the beach by the sand dunes. She does a cartwheel and, as she does so, her skirt drops over her head.

The boy from the hotel cafe is in board shorts now and runs down the sands to haul a dinghy from the water. When he strips off his shirt he does it without embarrassment, in one swift movement. And when he hugs the girl to him, his skin is the light gold of dry grass, the muscles of his upper arm flex and the tendons in his forearm stand taut and proud to his wrist, while the thick hairs on his legs catch in the sun.

This boy probably doesn't get good grades. This boy probably doesn't read such advanced books as he does. Instead, this boy will show his worth with his body. He will hold a woman and then his children. He will assert himself and know what to do.

He does not want this other boy to see him. He does not know why, only that he needs to keep watching, that this boy has something he wants.

The sun smashes on the surface of the water. And as

he hides there, behind the rock, a cloud passes over and covers him in shade, but when he looks up he can see no cloud, only the bright blue of the sky. And he feels overcome with shame at what he is doing, spying on this other boy, yet with an urgency unlike anything he has ever felt before.

What he wants to say is: make me good. Whatever it is that I lack, make me good. Make me normal. Make it so that I can be loved.

The other boy's hands are under the girl's top, upon her back. Their faces press together, his mouth on her neck and her hair is brushed over the other side so he can make out her face, her eyes closed. And they are no longer standing, at some point they've dropped to the sand, and they are twisting and moving, the hands at her back pressing her, molding her around him. A hand grabs at the thin fabric of her skirt and lifts it high above her waist, and only then does the young boy notice that the shorts of the older boy are lowered, that the top half of his buttocks are exposed, a pale ceramic next to his deep gold tan.

He hates this girl. He hates her more than the boy, this boy who is of the earth: made from sweat and leather and blood. But in some way he hates him too, as he consumes her as a horse does miles of open country.

And when they are finished, the couple part; the girl smooths her hair and skirt and the boy from the cafe pecks her on the nose. She takes the longest route back to the path, her footprints punctuating the sand. And the older boy watches her, as the younger boy watches him, and when she's gone, the older looks out to the sea and in one sudden movement he bounds into the water and arches into a dive.

And the boy—the other boy—swims out, his strokes strong and confident as he rides the waves, his arms and elbows flicking out, so arcs of light drop from his fingers as he raises his hands up into the air and then back down into the water. And of course this boy knows how to swim, this boy who lives on the islands, this boy who could be part fish. All the while the boy watches him from the shore, he wants to go in after him, to run down the sands and fall headlong into the water, but something holds him back.

And as the other boy continues to swim out, the sun breaking up on the surface, his body begins to wobble uncertainly in the deeper water, the arcs he draws grow smaller, the sound of his strokes quiet against the hush of waves upon the sand. The boy—the first boy—thinks he is going awfully far out. Should he call out?

He watches the head of the other boy grow smaller and smaller until he can only briefly see it, rising and falling, masked by the swell of the sea. And he keeps looking but now he can't see him at all, so he wonders whether he has just gone so far out he is imperceptible or whether the other boy has somehow disappeared. And at first he does not think very much, his mind has emptied in a way that he is immensely glad for after the tumult of before, as though the tide has come in and washed away all thought.

But then thought comes crashing back and he wonders: should he fetch help? The cafe is far away, the hotel even farther. He imagines running in, skinny and half-naked with gooseflesh. What would he say? And he imagines his voice, the same voice he was told to use to the landlord, piping them down to the beach. "I think a boy has been drowned," he'd squeak. So, no, he cannot go.

But there is no sign of the boy. He feels sure someone else will have seen, someone else will call and do something. But still there is no sign. And then he considers the other boy may be quite all right. But, if he is not, then it is only what this boy deserves: for having gone out so far, for what he did on the beach, for having it easy, for being blessed, for not having obeyed the rules, the rules that should apply to everyone.

As he scans the horizon, flat and sharp as a blade, the waves roll up the shore like reams of fabric spooling out of a machine. He stands and turns to go and finds the sand brittle beneath his feet. The sun is on his back as he walks up the dune, which crumbles and breaks beneath him, making his steps halting and uneven, like a stunned animal.

Finally, he runs through the grasses and breaks out onto the road, which opens out like a garden before him. And his breath comes hot and fast as he runs for the hotel, as he begins to wonder if the other boy hasn't drowned or disappeared but only turned while swimming out, turned without him noticing. Or even hauled himself out further up the beach. And he gets to wondering, and continues to wonder, to imagine, all the different versions, all the many possibilities, until almost convinced there had never been another boy at all.

Acknowledgments

Thank you to Louisa Joyner, Aisling Brennan, Rachael Williamson and Josh Smith at Faber, and Cal Morgan, Geoff Kloske and Alison Fairbrother at Riverhead. Also to my former PhD supervisors, Katherine Angel and Toby Litt, and also Julia Bell, all at Birkbeck, where this novel began.

Thanks also to Hawkwood in Stroud, for the residency where I finished this book, the Society of Authors for the grant that gave me time to write, as well as Writing West Midlands' Room 204 scheme for their mentoring and support.

Thank you to my friends, particularly those with whom I shared breaks in the British Library.

I wouldn't be here were it not for a few English teachers, who always encouraged me and were parents of another sort: Mike Craddock, Rosemary and Peter Diamond, and particularly Jinny Milton, who was the first one to get me writing and to teach me what it meant to write creatively. And also those who taught me without us being in a school: Dick Lane and Jonathan Lumby.

Finally, thanks to my agent, John Ash, who believed in me and this book; to my sister, Elizabeth; and to Aaron, for all his love and support.